Kingston upon Hull City Libraries
WITHDRAWN
FROM STOCK
FOR SALE

HULL LIBRARIES

ENTWINED

A novella by Zoe Miller

authorHOUSE®

AuthorHouse™
1663 Liberty Drive, Suite 200
Bloomington, IN 47403
www.authorhouse.com
Phone: 1-800-839-8640

© 2009 Zoe Miller. All rights reserved.

No part of this book may be reproduced, stored in a retrieval system, or transmitted by any means without the written permission of the author.

First published by AuthorHouse 3/23/2009

ISBN: 978-1-4389-5365-6 (sc)

Printed in the United States of America
Bloomington, Indiana

This book is printed on acid-free paper.

Dedicated, in loving memory, to my Una for always being there pushing me to write, and to the friends that have been both inspiring and supportive.

Contents

Home *1*
The Gift *9*
Prize Fight *13*
Obituary *23*
Second Chances *33*
Bend. *55*
In Search Of. *69*
Arrangements *73*
Secret Lives. *93*
Delivery *103*
Fluctuating Movements. *113*

Home

> *Life is a test of divine design. Faith is the No. 2 pencil with which we take the Test, and the Word is the answer book we can reference to pass the Test. However, if we lack faith we cannot take the Test, and if we are ignorant of the Word how can we pass? Yeah, life is a grand Pass or Fail Test. When the Test time is over, we can only hope that we read the Word right and our faith filled in the bubbles correctly. Then the Lamb will call out your name to hand out the reward for making the grade.*
>
> *~ Street Poet, autumn 2000*

Taylar closed the composition book of recorded quotes to look at the time. Kayla was late, and it was too hot to be outside. Sitting beneath the cloudless bright sky seemed to worsen the heat and sense of anticipation. The train station had emptied leaving the lonely hum of machinery. Trapped in the lull between trains and transients Taylar felt out of place; too exotic for the desert population that also called this place home. A mock turtleneck, long banded hair, paint-splattered jeans, and thong sandals were a far cry from the western gear normally seen in these parts. Taylar would have preferred to bypass this place and head further west, maybe to the ocean. The bay of San Francisco or the rainy streets of Seattle were more inviting. But Taylar had stopped here, unable to resist the urge to see the desert blossom.

The screeching of tires and the blaring horn brought Taylar out of revelry. The window of the halted Jeep rolled down revealing the crazed driver behind the wheel. Taylar did not bother to listen to the apology yelled out. After tossing the duffel bag into the back, Taylar eases into the passenger seat.

"Still as androgynous as ever I see," Kayla said. "Are you ever going to decide?" She peeled out of the station.

"Sure I will, the moment, you stop dyeing your hair," Taylar replied coolly.

Kayla came to a jerking stop at the next light, "Your parents wrote me."

"What did the neurotic alcoholic and fat-ass want?"

"Despite their flaws, prodigal child, they are your parents, and you should give them a call every now and again. Scottsdale isn't far. We can drive up there. Just like the old days."

"No, thanks" Taylar's voice was as dry as the air around them.

"Oh yeah, I almost forgot," Kayla said. "They've adopted again, a little girl from China this time."

"Poor kid, she should run as soon she can."

Kayla gave Taylar and irritated look. For ten years, she had been listening to Taylar whine about how horrible it was living with the Niancas. Taylar had runaway from home more than a dozen times, before reaching the age of sixteen. If the state had had its way Taylar would have been sent to boot camp, but Mr. Nianca had been able to convince Social Services otherwise. However, none of those events had any effect on Taylar. Six months later, the wayward teen had wound up in Tucson and attached to Kayla.

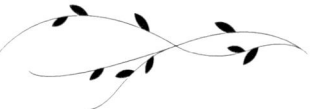

Kayla had just finished her third year at the Hardaway Institute and was going to celebrate with a quiet meal at home. Coming out of the grocery store, she wasn't paying much attention to her surroundings as she loaded the bags in her jeep. That mistake almost sent her into cardiac arrest when voice from behind shouted, "Don't move."

Obediently, she remained still, unable to think until she heard a snap. She missed the camera's flash because she had closed her eyes in fear.

"I wish you hadn't done that." The voice behind her groaned with disappointment. "The picture came out all wrong."

Kayla slowly turned her head to confront her assailant. She had not expected to find that a teenager had held her hostage with a camera. Enraged by this prank, she roared, "What's the matter with you? Get out of here before I call the cops!"

The teen looked from the scowling woman to the Polaroid, as if trying to decide which image was more profound. A contemplative look quickly developed into an impish grin.

"Since you've ruined my picture, you must let me sketch you live." Almond brown eyes stared into Kayla's as a chalk stained hand shoved the Polaroid into a pocket. Kayla felt hypnotized by the teen's expression. The warm gaze was so intense that she soon forgot that she had been afraid. The clanking and crashing of shopping carts brought her careening back to reality.

The situation was beyond believable, Kayla thought. Some random art student wanted her picture. It was too much. It had to be some kind of joke. She analyzed the face before her—long, dark hair, lean form, and a face too pretty for a young man, but an attitude too brash for a young woman. Either way, this person was probably barely legal. Therefore it had to be a joke. She had planned a quiet evening of dinner with smooth vodka to wash it down, then a nice, warm bath. This kid interrupted her plans.

"You should go about your business, kid. I don't have time for games."

The kid did not move. "My name is Taylar Nianca. I am very serious about painting you."

Kayla did not answer. She finished loading her bags into her car. Something about the kid's eyes said she would be missing out on something interesting if she refused. Maybe it was insanity. Maybe it was vanity. Whatever the reason, she took Taylar home on that hot summer afternoon. The series of sketches done that week still grace her mantel.

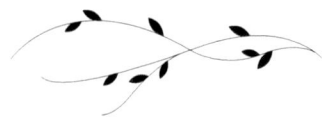

Today, it didn't take them long to get back to Kayla's subdivision, and for that Taylar could not have been happier. An early arrival meant escaping a lecture.

"Is everything still the same?"

"Yeah," she said. "Just more cluttered."

"I'm going to open up the attic." Taylar dragged the duffel behind the screen door.

"When do you plan on leaving?" she asked, slinging her bag and keys into a chair in the corner.

Taylar stopped at the bottom of the steps. "When I get my muse back."

"Just remember to lock the door, when you leave. You forgot last time."

Taylar just smiled and proceeded up the stairs. Two weeks passed before they had another semi-normal conversation.

Kayla tossed and turned in the heat, wide awake and sweaty. The ceiling fan whirled overhead, but it was not enough to cool the night's hot air. The clock on the wall said that morning was nowhere in sight. It gave Kayla a glimmer of hope that deep sleep might come between now and then. Reaching for the glass on her nightstand, she found no refreshment, forcing her to go to the kitchen for more water. The smell of smoke filled her nostrils. *Taylar's smoking, that's why the house is sweltering,* she thought. In a childish effort to vent the fumes, her guest had turned off the A/C and opened the windows, but the night breeze was not strong enough to push the smog out.

The back door of the kitchen was also open, illuminating the linoleum floor. She opened the refrigerator and stood in front of it for moment, cooling herself before refilling the glass. Reluctantly, she closed the refrigerator and followed the path of light to the patio.

"What's troubling you?"

Taylar's head tilted back into an awkward pose, not to the side or slightly twisted around, but bent backward so that Kayla could look into the eyes she knew so well.

"Who is she?" Taylar's cigarette pointed to a canvas propped between two patio chairs. Kayla looked over the rim of the glass, pretending to examine the image. She knew what was about to happen. Taylar's version of twenty questions: where was I, what was my inspiration, what year was it, and so on. Unfortunately, she did not have the mental capacity to endure it tonight.

"How should I know?" she replied. "You painted her. You tell me."

The dark head went back up as Kayla sank into the opposite chair. "I think this was from when I was with that traveling circus," Taylar said. "But I didn't think I kept anything from that tour. Did I even talk about this chick?"

"You talk about a lot of people, especially your patrons."

"Whoever she is, she wasn't a patron. A muse, maybe...."

They sat in silence as smoke and warm air swirled about them. As Taylar's cigarette burned to the end, its ashes fell harmlessly on faded jeans. Kayla dozed off in the summer night as Taylar extinguished the butt. The scraping of plastic on concrete roused Kayla from her doze and she sleepily watched the painter and canvas disappear into the house. She listened to the sounds of the air conditioner starting up and closing windows, but she made no effort to move.

"You should come inside," the artist called to her. "Your bed's more comfortable than a lawn chair. I'm going to go paint."

Kayla sleepily followed the summons, but instead of sleeping in her bed, she dreamed the night away in the attic studio.

The Gift

For Millie Johnson, Wednesday was proving to be more stressful than Monday. Her desk piled high with CDs, proposals, manuscripts, and literary resources hid her glorified word processor. Despite all the items demanding her attention, she sat analyzing her e-mail, pondering the order in which to open them. Most of her e-mail was ignorable: corporate memos (she had all ready seen the rough drafts) and messages from clients who had to a million questions. The final category was the daily rant from Charlene. Only one title held her attention: FWD.FWD. NEW INTERN CANIDATE. The word "intern" was enough to give her a migraine.

Memories that came to mind from her days as an undergrad made her cringe. Those were the days when working with a mentor to gain experience really meant indentured servitude. The thought still conjured a bittersweet taste in her mouth. But Millie did not want to project her bad experiences on to someone else, so she scanned the file, looking for insight into the character of Deshawn Clemons. She was looking for something of substance, beyond grades or glowing reviews from pet professors. If this was just a random decision on this Mr. Clemons' part, she didn't want anything to do with him. She had worked hard to be "a *credit to the* community," just like Mother wanted her to be, and she'd be damned if she had to deal with some kid who was just killing time. But if this *Deshawn* showed any real interest in the work he might do, she would bend over backwards to help him.

The entire process just gave her a headache. She had already endured two clueless and unwilling interns this year and wasn't sure she could cope with a third. The worst part of all was that Funderburke would dump the intern on her. "You have the best people skills," he always said. It was a weak cop-out.

Millie started making a mental list of the preliminary information she would instill into her new underling. It was the rational thing to do, to prepare for the inevitable. Not that her job was rocket science, but it had its rules and regulations. Her internal debate is interrupted by the secretary and the delivery man, who was carrying a cardboard box that looked as though it had been stamped a thousand times.

"Oh...," said the secretary. "Sorry about barging in. I thought you had gone to lunch."

"I just took a short break," Millie replied.

The secretary signed for the package, and sent the delivery man on his way. Millie thought that would be it, but her secretary lingered in the office, intrigued by the over sized package.

"Aren't you going to open it?" she asked Millie.

"Not yet, Tanya. I have to get through this mountain."

Pausing for moment, Millie thought of everyone she knew that might have sent her a package. Normally, she did not receive anything this large. This unexpected delivery did not sit well with her.

"You never get anything this big," Tanya said. "Is it something you ordered online? I've never heard of TiPiNianca. What do they make?"

Millie wanted to laugh. "Order online? Me? You know me better than that. It's a miracle I can deal with e-mails. And I do not know any TiPiNianca."

"It's the name on the package. See?" Tanya pointed to the name with a long manicured fingernail. Millie got up from her desk to have a better look. Both women stooped in front of the package to read the return address. The sender's name was unfamiliar, and the P.O. box (a thousand miles away), even more unfamiliar.

"I have no idea who that is," Millie muttered, moving back to the safe confines of her desk. "Or what this is."

"You're not going to open it? Don't tell me you're not curious. Maybe it's from an admirer?" The look on Tanya's face made her look like a romance-obsessed teen.

"I'll wait until I can figure out where it came from."

"Aww, come on, Millie. Where's your sense of adventure?"

Millie just gave the secretary a harsh look over her reading glasses. "I think the phones are ringing," she said.

Tanya sighed. "Okay, but if you get curious, I'll gladly help you unwrap it." She ran out of the office in a gray blur, and Millie set about reorganizing her desk into a productive workspace. But first, she needed to respond to the e-mail. For a moment, she felt like a Caesar, holding someone's future in her hands. Thumbs down, and Deshawn Clemons would have to go to another department. Thumbs up, and she would have a new underling that could at least help get her inbox cleaned out. Millie's sense of benevolence won. She sent her thumbs-up response to the head editor.

After hitting the Send button, she glanced at the package still sitting in the chair in the corner. TiPiNianca would be on the back burner for a minute. *An unexpected package is nice*, she told herself, *but I'd like to know who it came from before I open it. That way, I know what to expect.*

Prize Fight

It was another Friday night in the underground garage, business as usual. The host sauntered about the pits, greeting his guests. Everyone here knew that golden smile. This evening, he was escorted by two big Doberman bitches, a gift from a seller he could not wait to see. Idly, he seized up the competition, putting his money here and there, for and against his own dogs. He was too suave to handle his own fighters, so he let his cronies do it. It was a big, profitable night for the host. Lots of planning went into getting all these sellers, buyers, owners, and spectators there to witness a blood sport.

Despite the location, the lights were intrusively bright, and the jewels of the high-rollers only made it worse. But for all their glamour and ruckus, these ballers would not be interrupted, not with all the palms that had been greased, and certainly not when they were tucked under a quarter mile of concrete and steel. Besides, why would anyone notice a barrage of cranked up cars headed into the city's center? After all, it was a beautiful night.

The invitation list was long, and not everyone was a friend. That meant all weapons were checked at the door. There was too much money to be lost if homicide came calling. Everyone was quickly but thoroughly frisked, green blips on the scanner. Access granted, down the elevator they go.

Here only two things were colder and harder than you: the concrete floor and the greenbacks that constantly change hands. But just because you made the list, this doesn't mean you earned safe passage. Scores were settled and debts were paid—dead presidents pending or dead man walking; choose your partner. But it was all good. They came to watch the match and gamble a bit. That's what Friday nights are for.

Ground level, off the elevator, and distinctive odors rushed at the guests: alcohol, cigar smoke, stale perfume, sweat. The metallic scent of blood and a dusty musk of dog hung in the air. The smell was so thick the body almost rejected the oxygen necessary to propel stubborn limbs into the adrenalin charged atmosphere. The M.C. was already shouting commentary over the microphone. He was a force unto himself, his voice carrying over the shouting crowd, and dogs barking and whining with excitement. Their rumble was contested only by the rattling dice of the gamblers huddled against the walls in Section AA, Spot 30. Loaded dice were rolling. There would be a good fight of the humankind before the night ended.

A newcomer caught the host's eyes. She seemed out of place in this bunch. The red hound on the leash was odd enough, but her walk, her talk were all wrong. But she had made the list. She was an acquaintance of the esteemed host, a breeder looking for promising specimens. Dressed for a power luncheon, she was here to do business with the dog men. 'Let's go' is blaring from the speakers as two Rottweilers went for each other and the dice kept rolling.

"Aisha! Baby girl, long time, no see!" As the host approached his guest, the hound hid behind his mistress's leg. The host leaned in close to embrace an old friend. "The albinos are at the rear," he said. "They won't fight for awhile. You should have enough time to look them over." He stepped back and gave her a flirtatious wink.

Another match started, and the owners were playing the dozens. The bulls were snorting and growling, itching to get going. Aisha made her way to the far pit, brushing off other sellers and drunkards. She ignored everything but the two isolated, locked, and chained kennels. Most fighters never left their dogs alone, but the master of these two dogs seemed to be MIA. Rumor had it that the owner of this pair shot anyone who came within six feet of his dogs. It was a good thing that security had all the weapons, although anyone with violent intentions didn't need a gun; a broken bottle worked just as well. The bull match ended in a short and rough victory. Full of energy, the M.C. rushed to begin the next match, hyping up the crowd with promises of a good brawl.

The puppy didn't want to be there. He was a pedigree, Westminster quality, Pharaoh. Why was he being subjected to this mongrel activity? Knowing the animal's apprehension, Aisha paused to consol him. "Trust your mama," she murmured. "Places like this build character." She patted his copper flanks and they moved deeper into danger. At seven feet from the kennel, Aisha could make out two snow-white dogs. At Six feet the albinos started barking. One dog circled in his cage, as if to gain momemtum to launch an attack. The other crouched and snarled. At five feet, Aisha knew she was in trouble when she felt a sharp poke in her side. The pup whimpered and started shaking, expelling the contents of his bladder. A mischievous smile shaped her lips.

"What do you want?" The bass of that threatening voice excited Aisha more than she wanted to admit. The edge of the glass cut high in her back. Her attacker was a tall man. The rumors were true. The calmest way to defuse the situation, Aisha told herself, was to stand perfectly still. It worked to calm most beasts. Sometimes the same technique worked on people. At this moment, she had few choices. She had no allies here, no protection, yet, she was excited. Aisha's exhilaration ran deeper than the pride of watching one of her whelps win its first match.

Adrenaline spread through her veins. *I don't miss this kind of high,* she said to herself, *but I need one of those dogs. I wish I hadn't smoked that joint.* She tried to think clearly, but her senses were going out of control, her vision blurred by the fluorescent lights. The chanting from the next fight rang in her ears. Her tongue was dry as sand, and the scent of her assailant filled her nostrils. The combined sensations only succeeded in making the glass pressed against her side feel painfully satisfying; resulting in her recklessness reaction of leaning into the makeshift weapon. She was sure he would pull it back. He was just bluffing to test her nerve. But, if he didn't back down; that glass was going to slide right into her chocolate-truffle skin.

"Step off, broad." The attacker tightened his grip and pressed a little harder, solidifying his promise. But, Aisha stood fast. Her tetanus was up to date, and, besides, she had two to five minutes to get help before she suffocated from the punctured lung. "I have a bitch I wanted mated," she said as calmly as possible. As he shifted, she felt his eyes examining her and the puppy. "Leave." He took some of the edge off his weapon, indicating she should escape. Instead she stood there wavering between staying and leaving. She decided to stay. She decided to play her river card. "Baja's Dobermans came from my kennel. He told me you bred that pair special. The one I have at home is special. You can examine her if you're interested."

"You the one he's been going on about?"

The next chain of events happened as expected. Some fighting broke out, who cheated, who stole, who lied, some dogs were put down, and others were stored way. Drunks were herded out, and the M.C. packed up his electronics. It was a very profitable night for Baja. The cleanup crew was coming in, and in a few hours the garage would be just another docking bay for Joe White-Collar and his Volvo.

Two vehicles separated from the early Saturday morning traffic of thrill seekers. A black van followed a champagne Cadillac out of the city's center. The hound stuck his head out the passenger window, grinning at the world as they floated by. Avoiding checkpoints, the Caddy left the skyline in the distance, exchanging it for the darkness of suburbia. Aisha checked her rearview mirror to make sure that she was being followed. She felt as giddy as a mad scientist. It had taken a long time to track those dogs, longer than she had expected. The rumors had not done them justice.

Turning into a gravel driveway, roll by the home that act like sentinel gaurding her secret. The Caddy came to a stop at the edge of the lot, where the tree line began. Aisha left the car, with the puppy following close behind. Sober in the night air, she signaled her guest to follow her deeper into the woods. The van's headlights illuminated the dirt trail, but Aisha didn't need the light; she has walked this track a million times. The van rolled into the bush, until she signaled him to stop and get out. Once attacker, now prospective partner, he stalked forward, and when he was close enough, she turned on the lights of her half-submerged compound. As they entered the waddle and daub kennel, some of the dogs began growling, but it didn't bother them. When Aisha asked the man what she should call him, he didn't reply. But she didn't care. He was interested, and that was all she needed to know. They passed a small office, on the way through the U-shaped kennel where she quickly deposited her Pharaoh in a vacant cage. In her giddiness, she began to brag that she was never able to keep more than fifteen dogs at a time. Mostly pit bulls, a few Dobermans, but her real passion was for the exotic. She went on to brag about her long list of clients and their demand for quality.

She stopped in front of an inhabited cage and let out a low whistle. A blue-gray bitch trotted forward. After unlocking the cage, Aisha grabbed the bitch's collar, inviting the stranger to inspect her. His hands quietly felt the dog's frame. This dog was strong and mature, but he was less than appreciative of her overly obedient temperament.

"Seems powerful, I'll give you that," he said, feeling over the dogs muscles. "This coat is a unique color and texture, a short course blue grey. You don't see that everyday. This head is huge, and wrinkled some kind of Molossoid type? How many breeds did you mix?" He stepped back for another look.

"Three," she said. "The progenitor, Max was already mixed: pit and Shar Pei. He was this color. I mated him with a grey Cane Carso. Then, I took a male, Otis from the first litter, and mated him with lilac Shar Pei. The first pair gave me another litter. Then I had an idea, mate one from Max's second litter and one from Otis's litter. I've been lucky. There have no defects. But I had all the others culled, and keep the two strongest. Only Doris and Dorian are left, one to breed for strength the other for intelligence. " Aisha rubbed the head of her treasure.

"What are you trying to Frankenstein? She's hardly aggressive. This beast is just an oversized mutt. You're wasting my time"

"Mutt!? Are you kidding me?! Doris is a beautiful hybrid, the perfect example of strength and obedience. I didn't breed her for the ring. I want her litter to be breed for power. I heard that your dogs are exceptional, from some people and, hoped you might be willing to share."

Aisha has begun petting the animal again subconsciously, admiring her creation. The only reason Doris was here and not in her own home was because it was easier to exercise and socialize her in the kennel. Other wise Aisha hated that her prize pet was so far from her. The hound that had accompanied her this evening was just for show, Doris was hands down her favorite.

"Your experiments don't interest me." Aisha looked away from the dog man. Doris had been keeping a weary eye on the visitor.

"A litter from this pair could create a new breed for home or ring. Your fighters look like hybrids to me. So how can look down your nose at mine"

Her guest paused before asking, "Is there anyone else involved in this project?"

"No one that would interest you."

He stoked his goatee, still thinking. "You keep records on this mutt?"

Without a word, Aisha locked her treasure away again and led her guest out of the kennel and back to the office. As she pulled a photo album from the top shelf, he sank into her desk chair, waiting to see the records. "You haven't told me what I'll benefit from this," he said.

She gave him a level stare. "How much do you want for a stud?"

He gave her a dispassionate snort. "I don't need your paper. You've approached others with this. What have they asked for?"

"Now who's wasting time?" Perhaps her high was wearing off now. Or maybe it was the way this man was trying not to be obvious about memorizing the things in her office. But the danger lights in her head were flashing bright red. As if they were in one of the pits they had just come from, they stared each other down.

"You look like the business type," he said, leaning back in her chair. "So I'll assume you know how this works. I have something you want. Now you make me an offer, preferably something I might want. I only came because I was curious. I'm not into breeding guard dogs."

She was getting angrier by the minute. Where had she hidden the Colt? The flashing red light in her mind pulsed faster. There was a metallic gleam coming from the shelf on her left hand side, just out of reach. *Found it!*

"Half the litter," she said, "and you can board your dogs here whenever you like."

"Better." He nodded. "Are all your clients given the same offer?"

"My associates have nothing to do with this deal." Her mental red light was flashing a mile a minute. She had been too excited about the call, too hyped that her project was near completion. She had missed the signs. This place would be undergoing renovations tomorrow. This civil servant thought he was going to get her to snitch, or, worse, pin her with something. *Note to self,* she thought, *the feds are now employing very attractive, smooth-talking, Micah Phifer look- a-likes.*

"I can't help but wonder," he was saying. "How did a corporate girl like you get involved with the likes of Baja?"

"I have no time for games," she snapped. "Either you're in or you're out."

The mole stood up from Aisha's chair. "I was hoping you would convince me that your cause was worth my time."

Aisha folded her arms. It was clear, the negotiations were over.

"If you find something that will interest me...." He crossed the room and slide a card into the waistband of her skirt, before exiting the room. When she heard the

Van start up, she vented her anger on her desk. Not that the solid punch did much damage, but what else could she do. She could not blame anyone but herself. She was on Fed Radar, and hitting one of their agents is a bad idea. Trouble, had come her way with a captial 'T'. That meant a big headache. She made some calls. By that afternoon, the kennel was underground. And as far as the house was concerned, she knew some good folks who could use the land.

Obituary

Deshawn paced around his apartment. The powers that be had decided that it should rain on his day off. He had just finished his mid-terms and had nothing to study for, and Millie had not assigned him any reference material to read. In short, he had nothing to distract him from the gloom he was feeling. Standing before his bookcase, he was wondering what to read. It was only a few more days before their anniversary date, and the weather certainly set the mood. Among the books on Deshawn's shelves, there was a hidden diary. This diary was by no means unique; it was merely a collection of musings, each page the testament of experiences that had left him a little wiser. Today, he pulled out the diary with ceremonial propriety and turned to the only page that has a date and a newspaper clipping stapled to it. He solemnly read the date, then the article, then his own melancholy rendition of his best friend's death.

Watcher did not see him die.

It doesn't matter,

Dead men are irrelevant.

Watcher observes a corpse, why?

Roll away limp form
Shrug it off, and forget it
In an avenue she slumps,
Witness granny's theft
Behind you, another victim
Battered and violated
All this in the rain
Tread home to suburbia
Stand before your door, watcher.
Do you hear the storm?
Thunderclouds hide ill intent
His keys in hand, coughing blood.
Officer, your perp
Has blended into the night.
So sad, mistaken watcher
Irrelevant, boy
Shot down in the dead of night

Every fall, Deshawn read this passage to himself as a reminder that he was living for two.

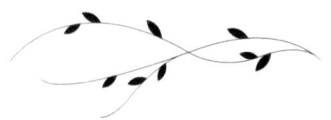

"I'm sorry, Mom. I can't make it to Mr. Gibson's funeral."

Holding the phone away from her ear, she half-heartedly listened to her mother whining about how ungrateful and self centered she was.

"Aisha, you owe that man," the woman on the other end said, still lamenting that she had raised such an ungrateful child.

Aisha's mother failed to realize that her youngest child hated the very idea of funerals. What was she to do? Stand there and cry as she watched his body being lowered into the ground? Mr. Gibson would love that. Aisha could hear his voice as clearly as if he were standing right next to her. "Aisha, stop ogling. Don't you have better things to do? You'll have enough time to laze about when you're dead!" Despite her mother's ranting, Aisha knew she respected the man. She owed him her life and career. Mr. Gibson was the father she wished she'd had.

She remembered meeting her so-called real father when she was very young. She hadn't thought much of him and was grateful he stayed away. She had her mom and the aunts. What did she and brother need with a father? Or any other male figure? That was until she hit puberty and lost her mind. Her older brother, Jeffery had gotten a scholarship to an out of state college, and was gone just as she was entering high school. Unlike her brother, she hated school. Following her cousin, Patches, she always ducked out on school to go boost and chill around the way. The spring Aisha turned fifteen, she found herself facing community service or juvenile hall. That was when, out of nowhere, her Aunt Tina brought Mr. Gibson to the sentencing. He said a few words on behalf of the family and offered his tax and financial services office as the site of her community service.

She was brought out of her revelry when she heard the F-word again. Come to think of it, Mr. Gibson hadn't even gone to his son's funeral. What was the kid's name? Jason? The old goat had said, "What can I do for a dead boy?" Aisha had snooped though his papers and found out that the son was from a failed marriage. The ex-wife wanted to be as far away as Gibson's money could get her. Gibson thought he was doing the right thing by staying away. Now there would be no reconnecting for him and his son because the kid had been killed shortly after his high school graduation. Under his workaholic exterior, however, Gibson was really torn up about it. Aisha supposed that his regret was her good fortune. He showed her the tricks of his trade to the letter and made sure she was a chartered accountant before she graduated from high school. He even convinced her to get an associate degree. Aisha definitely owed Gibson for teaching her how to be independent. The guilt started to set in. "Alright, Mama," she finally said. "I'll go to the wake."

Tanya's mentor, Beatriz Dixon, had left this world. Her father called her to tell her about the funeral. It seemed unreal to Tanya. How could Mrs. Beatriz die? Mrs. Beatriz had been both her mentor. But, as it often happens with mentors and students, the student grows up and goes away; and Mrs. Beatriz became the person Tanya called on holidays and special occasions. A funeral would qualify as a special occasion. Tanya decided that she would ask for time off to fly down and pay her respects. It would not be until she arrived at the church that Tanya would realize how hard the passing of Mrs. Beatriz would hit her.

Tanya returned to her hometown as quiet as a ghost. She stayed in her father's house. Only to have him give her a disappointed look, because she could only stay for two days. He explained that she would have to give his condolences to the family because he had to pick more hours at the plant. Tanya knew she would have to do that even without him asking. Her Old Man wasn't going. He didn't handle death well. His way of coping was to work more hours at the plant. As a little girl, dear old dad had gone to work and made sure he could pay the bills and bury her mother. But, otherwise he wasn't available. Thankfully Ms. Beatriz had stepped in, and helped raise Tanya into womanhood.

The familiar roads of home weren't as familiar as they should be and, Tanya almost lost her way to Mt. Zion A.M.E. She entered the church quietly, respectfully, and composed, at least until she saw that cold head. In an instant, she was inconsolable. Mrs. Beatriz had been Tanya's North Star. Who knew it could be so heart-wrenching not to be able to say thank you?

"Why are you gone?" Despite the stares and murmurs Tanya had given up her seat in the back pew to kneel in front of a mahogany casket. "You're always supposed to be here!"

Funerals are supposed to be quiet memorials for the dead. But somehow this bereaved tramp had found her way into their somber gathering, and she wailed more than the entire family. The ushers knew it would be best to let her cry and say good bye. "Let the young woman be," one of the old women whispered. "She ain't hurting a soul." The pastor continued his sermon, hoping his words of the blissful afterlife that had embraced their church mother, would give the mourners comfort. That was what they had hoped for when the first tearful sobs erupted from Tanya.

The congregation began to sing, "*Swing Low, Sweet Chariot*," and the pallbearers were approaching. Tanya had not let go of Beatriz's cold fingers. Before the bearers had to pull her away, someone called out to her. "Tanya?" The voice that called her was familiar. A sound so comforting and beguiling that it nearly brought her out of her grief.

Tanya vaguely remembered the round laugh lined face before her. The woman had the kind of face Tanya hoped she would have in old age; smooth brown and slightly lined. The matron's light brown eyes shone with wisdom and understanding, she even smiled. The kind of smile people give to those in mourning, the one where they are about to say something you may not want hear. "Tanya, it's time to let go."

But, this smile did not make Tanya feel worse. Maybe it was because this kind soul offered her a sincere measure of concern and sympathy. Gently, the woman pulled Tanya's fingers into her own hands and guided her away.

Tanya's tears subsided for a moment. Now that her vision was a little clearer she could think about who she was sitting with. The shock only added to her fatigue. It was Ms. Elly. Her father had called months ago and said that Ms. Elly had to be put in the nursing home, because she had lost her faculties. Contrary to that, here Ms. Elly sat as alert and vivacious as ever.

Then the casket was closed and hefted, initiating another flood of tears. Ms. Elly gave her a handkerchief. Studying the girl's sorrow, she waited for a pause between sobs to speak. "Bea talked about you the most," she said. "She worried about you a lot, her little lamb. She said you were too sensitive to things around you."

"She's dead."

"Only her earthly body is dead. Bea's soul has gone on to the Lord."

Tanya remained quiet as the church mother continued. "Bea spent her life doing what she was called to do. To work with you young people, was her calling. A lot of y'all turned out fine. Some were just taken by the devil."

"She was the original life coach," Tanya finally said. "A real positive influence, kept me grounded, taught me to be a lady. All that stuff they talk about in after-school specials. There aren't too many like Mrs. Beatriz out there anymore."

"Why don't you take up her yoke? Continue her good works. It might do you and someone else some good."

Feeling like she had heard the voice of the Holy Spirit, Tanya gaped at the woman holding her hands. Until that very instant, she felt as though she had been on the right track. One simple suggestion shifted and remolded everything she had thought was supposed to make her complete. She hugged Ms. Elly, and said what she had been unable to say to Beatriz Dixon.

"Thank you."

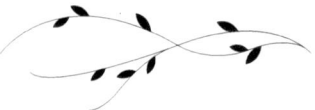

"Good morning, Tanya," said the person approaching Tanya's desk.

"Good morning, Ms. Georges. Here are your messages."

Tanya appeared to be oddly rejuvenated. Just two days ago, she had pleading for the day off. Tanya's boss marveled at her and wondered if she had been hoaxed.

"I thought somebody had died, the way you carried on the other day," Charlene Georges said as she flipped through the papers in her hand. "Are you sure you are all right?"

Tanya was hoping that she could avoid talking about what happened with her tactless boss. At least Millie had the decency to respect her privacy. "My Godmother died," was all she said.

"You have my condolences.… What's this?" Charlene pulled a pamphlet out of her stack. It was from the local youth mentoring agency.

"Sorry. That's mine." Tanya hastily reached over to retrieve it.

A penciled eyebrow went up. "It's amazing," Charlene said. "Amazing what death can do for the living."

Tanya sat there, quietly fuming at this callous woman. It was too early in the morning for banter. Thankfully, Deshawn appeared at just the right moment, saving her from the editor's snide commentary on life and death.

"Hello there, you must be Charlene. I am Deshawn Clemons, the new intern," he said extending his hand.

"Humph. The new apprentice. Tanya, I'll be in my office for the rest of the day." Charlene Georges sauntered away, humming some Disney song, without shaking his hand.

"That evil whi—"

"Don't say it," Tanya warned him. "Don't even think it. She's not evil. Just a little crazy."

"By crazy, you mean menstrual? Or crazy, as in loony bin-bound?"

Tanya was reorganizing her cluttered desk. "The second. Millie says I should dismiss anything she says that isn't work related."

"With an attitude like that, it must be hard."

"She's brilliant and tolerable when it comes to work. It's only difficult when she decides to be social. Mr. Funderburke is supposedly the one who got her out. And he's the only man she will talk to. So stay clear."

"Just when I was beginning to think it would be okay to work in an office full of females."

Second Chances

"Let me die. Let me die," the woman whimpered from her bed as nurses and orderlies converged on her. The orderlies had to drag her from the bathroom and hoist her unto the bed. One was checking her vital signs, while others were struggling to get the tubes for the stomach pump into her mouth.

The woman hurt, hurt everywhere, body, mind, and soul, all at once. She was ready to let go. She was ready for the hurting to stop. Living just hurt too damn much. It was her memories of what she had gained that were the source of her sadness. Her American dream would not fade away. There was nothing that would make the emptiness inside her go away, trying to move on only seemed to make the pain worse, and the world was more frightening because of her fear of pain. Living in fear was just as bad as living in sorrow. She was a woman who had lost everything. There was only one thing left to dispose of: her life.

"Mrs. Brighton? Mrs. Brighton, can you hear me?" The doctor flashed his pen light at her dilated irises.

Despite all the anguish she thought she had already endured, her body seemed to want to endure a little more. She heard the call of the man trying to pull her back from death.

"Harris, are you sure you want to take this patient on?" Frustration filled the chief psychologist's voice. "Mrs. Brighton has been here for years, most of that time on suicide watch. She has also proven to be the most obstinate and unresponsive person here."

"I am well aware of that, Dr. Stephens," the new resident at Hardaway Institute said. "I've been through her file several times. I think if we change our approach, we may be able to make some progress."

Dr. Kayla Harris was rather young for the profession, but she came with astounding accolades from former professors and employers. Hardaway was in need of "fresh blood," as the administrators put it, but what they really needed was more funding. The only way to get it was to show that Hardaway was a progressive and lucrative institution, not just a nursing home for the mentally unstable. Administration had thus decided to the update the institution's treatment methodology. Many believed that personal attention would be the new prevailing wind in treatment. But Stephens was old school. He believed in the power of pharmacology and was leery of this so-called New Age medicine. Kayla was New Age from the way she walked and talked to her *Clairol* red locks. Stephens disliked her on sight. He decided he would test the new resident by letting her have one pet project in addition to her regular patients. This pet project would be treated with the new methodology and would have to show substantial change in time for Harris's one year review. Mrs. Brighton was the last patient he expected her to choose.

Kayla had chosen Alice Brighton for one simple reason: her method was designed for this type of patient, for the ones that were hiding from the world.

"All right, Dr. Harris," said Dr. Stephens, "you can begin your sessions with the patients tomorrow. Good luck."

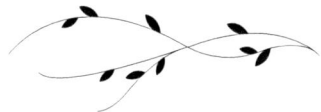

Mrs. Brighton was sitting in her dark room, listening to the sounds of the morning. According to Mrs. Brighton, everything started at dawn. She was mildly surprised to hear a tap at her door. It was still early for rounds to begin. She didn't move. Whoever it was would enter, no matter what she said.

"Good morning, Mrs. Brighton," An unfamiliar voice chirped. "Can I come in? The floor nurses said you are usually awake at this hour. The sunrise must be lovely" The unfamiliar doctor made her way to the windows. "Let me open the blinds for you, it's a beautiful morning."

"Don't open them!"

The doctor paused in front of the window. "All right. May I at least turn on the light?"

"If you must."

The doctor flicked the light switch filling the room with a soft artificial glow of fluorescents. "I am Dr. Kayla Harris," she said to the old woman in the bed. "You can call me Kayla."

The resident only arched her eyebrow. "Humph," she said. "You are woefully young for that title."

"Do you want breakfast?" Kayla asked, ignoring Mrs. Brighton's insult.

"What breakfast? The kitchen isn't open yet."

Kayla shrugged "All I know is that there's food downstairs. If you want it, Alice."

"Toast and coffee will be fine."

"That's it? They have real food. I mean, like bacon and eggs kind of food."

"It's too early for all that."

"Okay, then, when I come back, we'll have a chat."

As Kayla passed the nurses' station, a group of nurses stopped her.

"Well?" they asked her. "Tell us what happened."

"Nothing happened. Excuse me. I'm going to get Mrs. Brighton and myself some breakfast." As she walked to the elevator, she could still hear them talking.

"Boy," said one nurse, "does she have her work cut out for her with that one."

"Yeah," said another nurse. "I heard her own kids put her in here and haven't seen her since."

"Yeah, Brighton's mean alright," said a third. "You're lucky you haven't seen one of her episodes."

Hoping to glean some useful information about the patient, Kayla paid close attention to what these chatterboxes were saying. She had studied the notes in Mrs. Brighton's chart, but the notes were only clinical observations. Those renditions were generic and lacked the insight of candid personal opinion. Committing the nurse's conversation to memory, the doctor could wait to find out how much of it turned out to be factual or plain gossip. At best, she might even witness some of the patient's habits this morning.

When Kayla returned, Mrs. Brighton was sitting in her rocker, humming and staring at the blank wall. Setting the breakfast tray on a serving table, the doctor leaned against the far wall to look around the room, hoping to find a clue into what made Alice Brighton a patient and not an active member of society. *"She has a private room,"* the doctor noted, *"and personal clothing, plastic flowers, and a homemade quilt. It feels phony. She doesn't seem connected to anything around her. Nothing in the room is indicative of institutionalization or a person in transition."* Her thoughts were broken by the sound of the older woman's voice.

"If you are looking for a tip, forget it. This is not a hotel."

Kayla's expression became more focused. "The nurses think you're meaner than a rattlesnake. I wonder why?"

"Indeed."

"You have an interesting accent. Where are you from?"

"If you are in fact a doctor, there ought to be files at your disposal to give you that information."

"I'd rather ask."

Mrs. Brighton shrugged and sipped her coffee. "Why are you really here, Dr. Harris?"

"I just wanted to get to know you. I'll be your new counselor."

"You're a counselor? Not therapist or psychiatrist?"

"Correct."

Mrs. Brighton set the coffee down and eyed the young doctor leaning against the wall. "You're here to prove something," she said. "I am not inclined to help. The med nurse will be arriving soon. You should leave."

Kayla scribbled a note on her pad and said she would talk to her patient in a formal session another day. Once outside, she found the head nurse dispensing the morning medications to the residents of Hardaway.

"Dr. Harris," the nurse said, "how is your first day going so far?"

"So far, so good, Nurse Evans."

"That's good. If you'll follow me, I'll show you the rest of this wing and how we operate."

"Thanks. I would appreciate that."

"You were lucky she was in an accommodating mood this morning. Usually, we have to dodge anything we give her."

"Really? She is currently on a regimen of lithium, Nardil, and placidyl. She should be in a subdued state all the time."

The nurse gave Kayla a look of disbelief. "I don't think that woman has taken a full dose of that regimen in four years"

"Are you sure? How has she managed that?"

The nurse shrugged. "We can't prove that she doesn't take them, because her lab work always says the drugs are in her system." The nurse handed water and some barbiturates to another resident.

"I heard one of the nurses mention her episodes," Kayla said. "Her chart mentions sporadic behavior, from being quite and withdrawn to viciously aggressive."

"That about sums it up," the nurse said. "It happens daily in the spring."

"Interesting. Good thing I have two seasons to work on that. Is there anything else I should know?"

"Stay away from her curtains."

The rest of the day continued uneventful, and at the end of the day, Kayla sat down at her computer to record her notes. She had noticed that most of her patients were overmedicated. She decided immediately to decrease their dosages in order get a better understanding of how best to treat them, individually. She worked on Mrs. Brighton's case last, especially since she wanted to devote a lot of time to her special case. It was obvious that Brighton had a lot of mental barriers and phobias brought on by depression. Mrs. Brighton had no previous history of mental illness, but had had a mental breakdown of some sort and not recovered. Kayla's course of action would be simple: she would talk the woman down and get her off the meds.

Three days later, an orderly walked Mrs. Brighton into Dr. Harris's office for their private session. The doctor noted with curiosity the hateful look in the patient's cold glare.

"Good afternoon, Mrs. Brighton."

"Good afternoon," The apathy in her patience's voice worried the doctor.

Kayla frowned. "Where would you like to begin today? Anything you want to talk about, Alice?"

"On friendly terms so soon, even though I've declined to help you, with your designs for greatness?"

"I don't know about greatness," Kayla gently replied. "I just want to help people."

Mrs. Brighton pushed her hair behind her ear with an air of indifference. "That is very noble of you. Tell me, how you can help anyone if all you know is in black and white?"

"I can tell you have a certain disdain for that orderly."

"And a crow has wings."

"Why are you being defensive, Alice?"

"My happy pill quota has been altered. Am I a stone or a guinea pig?"

Kayla was quiet for a moment as she thought of the best response. An inexperienced therapist might analyze what Alice had just said, playing into the distraction. "I would have you be neither," the doctor finally replied. "But if you are one or the other, the lithium and the Nardil are doing little to help you, so you don't need them. Therefore, you are not a stone, neither are you stoned. However, the reduction in the pacidyl dosage should not induce defensive behavior. Besides I am not testing you for side effects, thus you are not my guinea pig. So, I ask again, why are you being defensive?"

When she asked the question again, Kayla expected a change in body language, something bordering on violence, or perhaps passive surrender. However, all she received was a glassy eyed stare from her patient.

"A tower defends nothing, it merely watches," Alice began to recite. "And a guard is just a guard. Where have all the knights gone?"

"Riddles and poetry do not an answer make, Alice. It seems that you enjoy using wordplay to hide yourself. You don't have to have to hide from me."

There was an odd rhythm in their conversation, as if they were dancing with words.

Had Kayla not been carefully observing her patient, she would have missed the slight smirk that graced her patient's thin lips. That was the last visible response that the doctor received. Her patient had closed herself off. Guessing that Mrs. Brighton might like literature, Kayla used her laptop to search the Internet for works of poetry, starting with the classics, then the modern greats like Hughes, Frost, and Angelou, which she read aloud. The counseling session became a one sided recital as Alice maintained her indifference. As the hour came to a close, Kayla leaned back in her chair and gave a defeated sigh. The same orderly who had escorted Mrs. Brighton to the session rapped at the door. The old woman rose stiffly from her chair as the door was pushed open. She took a step, and then stopped.

"Have you ever read 'Rumplestilzskin' Doctor?"

"Not since childhood."

"Tell me my name, Dr. Harris, and I will consider answering your questions." The older woman padded out of the office; leaving a very confused doctor to ponder her parting words.

Kayla felt so defeated that she leaned back in her, staring at the ceiling. Another tap on her door brought Kayla out of her daze.

"That looks very productive, Dr. Harris."

"Oh, hello, Dr. Stephens, what can I do for you?"

The doctor gave her a phony smile. "Just came to check on you."

"Thank you. Dr. Stephens, I have a question about Mrs. Brighton. Has she ever shown any signs of dissociative disorder? I have read and reread her chart, but her behavior is nothing like what I expected."

Dr. Stephens stepped further into the room and shut the door behind him. "Dr. Harris, you are new to this field. I want to give you some advice. There are patients here who need to be here, and there are some who don't. Some were put here because someone else mandated that they be here. And a few are here because they choose to be. Therefore, as doctors we must choose wisely who to focus our energy on."

"Are you saying I shouldn't focus on Mrs. Brighton, because of her history?"

"I'm saying that there are other patients who would benefit more from your treatment methods than Alice Brighton"

Dr. Stephens left Kayla in an even more defeated state than he had found her in. She had been on the job only a few weeks and seemed to be hitting roadblocks at every turn, with the Brighton case. Her others patients seemed be doing better with the changes in their medications. The Nurse was doing their best to adjust her methods, and some had already commented on the positive effects. Although a number of her patients did need the medication in addition to constant supervision, Mrs. Brighton was not in that percentile. Alice Brighton needed something else that Kayla could not put her finger on just yet.

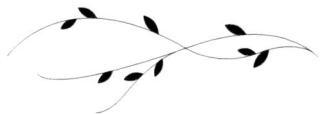

"Good morning, Mrs. Brighton. I brought you some coffee."

Kayla was as cheerful as ever, but her cheer did little to change her patient's haughty disposition.

"It has been three days," the old woman said. "What have you to say to me?"

Kayla sipped her coffee and nodded, "About that, it dawned on me that Brighton is probably your married name, so I assume you would prefer to be called by your maiden name. The story you mentioned was written by the Grimm brothers. So your name is Alice Grimm."

Alice rolled her eyes and stirred her drink "To err is human."

Kayla had been proud to have come to that conclusion on her own, but her ego was dealt a mild blow by the patient's reaction. "You answer to the name Alice. That must be your first name."

"Can a rose be anything other than a rose, if you call it by another name?"

"You are talking in circles."

"Am I? That would be foolish."

Kayla was finding that Alice had succeeded in irritating her. She had only come to her room in the hope of getting a better dialogue going. The last thing the doctor wanted was a repeat of the mime act that had taken place in her office.

"A fool is a prodigy in disguise," she replied. "We can carry on this banter for the rest of the morning, Mrs. Brighton, but that is not productive."

"I have all ready informed you that I am not inclined to help you."

Kayla chuckled, contriving a means gain control the conversation. "That is, unless I tell you your name." There was a long pause, and all Kayla heard was the sound of her own swallowing. In the dark room, she could hardly see the steel grey eyes boring into her. "The med nurse will be coming with my Lithi—"

"No, she won't," Kayla cut in. "You don't need it in the morning. You're very calm and relaxed during this time of the day. You need it in the afternoon. To keep you relaxed for your group therapy."

"I don't have group therapy."

"You do now. I think it will help you." Kayla watched Alice raise her cup as if to throw it. "I recommend against doing anything hasty," she said. "There are three big burly orderlies outside, and they'll rush in here to restrain you if they hear anything out of the ordinary."

Alice sat back in her rocker "Dr. Kayla Harris, you may be the good fairy in this fairy tale, but I will not be outdone."

Kayla blinked at the patient's strange refusal. In the blink of the eye, Alice moved so quickly that Kayla had barely enough time to dodge the rain of hot coffee. The splatter made streaks on the wall, and droplets showered her white coat. But Kayla didn't see the coffee stains. She had curled into a defensive position as the once docile hands of her patient changed into menacing claws.

Although Alice was not in the best physical shape, she was fast, and she took advantage of the doctor's instinctive dodge. Just as she had been warned, the orderlies came charging in when they heard the doctor's yelp. The men lifted the raging patient off the doctor as if she were a bag of flour. The charge nurse ran in behind the orderlies, a syringe and vial of sedative in her hands. Once the patient was sedated and restrained, Nurse Evans turned to the cowering young doctor. "Are you all right, Dr. Harris?" Green eyes shone in the dim light, showing a mixture of fear and shock. "You have just been assaulted by your patient," the nurse continued, "with only a scratch to show for it. You should report this to Dr. Stephens."

Kayla rose, mechanically obedient. She felt shaky, upset that she had let her guard down. But she had not expected the old woman to be so fast. Now she dreaded telling her superior what had happened. It was her fault. She had pushed the patient too far. Kaila was so distraught about it that when she reported to Dr. Stephens, he told her to take a longer lunch. It was clear from her attitude that Alice Brighton had won Round 2 of their on-going battle. She would be confined and restrained for a month. Kayla had a suspicion that Alice had known this would happen. Alice knew that an attack would keep her out of group therapy.

Kayla felt conflicted about Mrs. Brighton's punishment. She was a doctor, not a jailer. But what could she do? Rules were rules, and Alice was not above them; even if she was very good at manipulating to rules to accommodate, to her wants. Kayla planned to revisit her patient, but before doing so, she looked again at her personal records to get a better idea of who she was before she came to Hardaway. The text simply said, "Divorcee: all claims sent to Mr. Douglas Brighton." It took an Internet search to find the details in a report from the local newspaper: 'Local author has mental breakdown.' The article reported that an "up and coming writer" had suffered "a mental breakdown due to sudden and bitter divorce from her husband of thirteen years, Douglas Brighton, producer and entrepreneur." Mrs. Brighton had been sent to Hardaway Institution for evaluation. That had been eight years ago. The judge ordered that Douglas Brighton pay her medical bills as alimony. She felt confident that now she was armed for tomorrow's battle. Turning the computer off, Kayla went home with a faulty assumption.

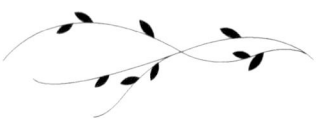

"Dr. Harris, how good of you to visit," Alice sang out, her voice filled with sarcasm. "That scratch has healed nicely. I was worried you got an infection or something." Kayla sighed into her coffee, embarrassingly conscious of an invisible red line on her left cheek.

"Shouldn't Stephens be here to scold me or something?" Alice purposely rattled her restraints.

Kayla strolled over to thick drapes and began toying with the hem of fabric. "Rumplestilzskin was a pixie of sorts, wasn't he, Alice?" Kayla waited for an answer she knew would not come. "All of those fairy creatures loved the light. They even did their dirty work in the day."

"What is your point?"

"Your vampire-like tendencies don't match your fey self-image" Kayla said, looking at the closed curtains.

"My dear girl, what a thing to say?! This is a psychiatric facility. You should watch your language." The old woman gave a sinister chuckle.

"Lady, this is not some literary contest. It's real life."

Alice smiled. "When I was a little girl, my father would talk about life like it was a joke. Then if he was being serious he would say, 'You think these jokes? It's real life.'"

"You know what your problem is?" Kayla said. "You're angry and bitter, and a list of other things I can't think of right now. But just because some man abandoned you, that doesn't mean you get to abandon yourself and hide from the world. That's just pathetic."

"Well, now, isn't this a well-versed analysis. This is out of character for you, isn't it Dr. Harris. Did someone get under your skin today?"

"I will make a deal with you, Alice. Attend a group counseling session twice a week. You don't have to speak when you go. I just want you to behave yourself and get out of this room. The orderly will go away, and a female nurse will be assigned. No more restraints and I'll take you off the lithium and Placidyl. "

"How am I to endure without the white knight? Sir Tighty-Whiteys, my gracious captor. No, he must remain forever at my side. He shall accompany me always," Alice crooned with melodramatic fever. "Even as I go hither to yon privy."

The male nurse stood off to the side, ignoring the banter.

"Please, Alice, do this for me."

Alice glazed at the doctor with owlish expression. "Why?"

"Because…. Because…," Kayla struggled for a compelling comeback. "We both know this is not what you need. You can't honestly want this."

Alice yawned and leaned back into her pillows. "Sir Tighty-Whiteys, methinks the maiden dost jest. Look, how earnestly she doth imply she knows my nature. And yet she knows not my name. Come, fair maiden, and tell me my name, then I may grant ye a word."

Unable to tolerate Alice's mocking mood, the doctor left her patient. They had come to another stalemate. All of her efforts were being met with theatrical resistance. Alice was so deep in her self-pity that the young doctor was at a loss for how to break down the barriers she had erected around herself.

The public library soon became Kayla's second refuge. It was where she could work at the riddle that was Alice Brighton. For, six months, she had been questioning her sanity for indulging in Alice's delusions. She realized that the name issue was one thing that Alice had become obsessed with during the last year. A proper name could be the one thing that stood between failure and success with Alice Brighton. So here Kayla sat, reading and re-reading every fairy tale she could find. Beside the stacks of books was a notebook in which she was recording all the cross-references between Alice and fairy tales. But her conclusions and the lists she was making seemed ridiculous. Then, just as she was packing up for the night, she caught a glimpse of something familiar. The library clerk was shelving the afternoon's returns in the children's section. The little green book on the top of the pile was the written version of Alice's delusion. Kayla picked up the book and started flipping through the pages. At the very back she found the missing piece to her puzzle.

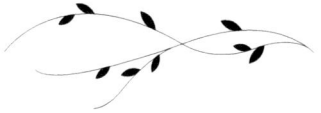

"What did you say?" The patient stopped mid-sip when the doctor placed the picture book in her lap.

"I read about what happened to you, Charlene Georges. You were born in the U.S. Virgin Islands in 1961. You migrated to the States in 1976. Charlene published her first book and married in 1979. In 1992 you were divorced and admitted to Hardaway."

"Oh. That. It makes for a great tragedy. Don't you think so? A story told a thousand times over." Noticing the impatient look on Kayla's face, she stopped talking for a minute.

"Do you want to tell me, your version of what happened?" Kayla asked. "The papers make it seem like Georges was a pseudonym."

Charlene gently stroked the cover of the book as if it were a delicate treasure. The usual sharp tongue retreated as she recounted her history. "Hardly," she said. "Alice Brighton is the pseudonym. My husband thought my real name was too ethnic. Charlene Alicia Georges. That is what my mama named me. I married him and became Alice Brighton. I had to forget that I grew up among mango trees. Then I lost my taste for curry and black cake, to feed is his aspirations. That was two years after I had Aaron."

"That's enough for today," the doctor said. "You don't have to tell me everything at once. I'll make sure the rest of the staff calls you Ms. Georges from now on."

"Kayla, will you open the curtains?" It was the first honest request Charlene Georges had made in years.

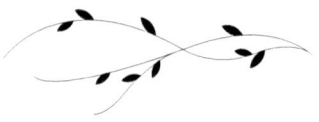

Their sessions were much smoother after that. Kayla was able to talk to Charlene about the reasons for her pseudo-insanity and the reality of her depression. She also managed to pair a treatable schizophrenic girl with Charlene, and somehow they helped each other. Now that she had regained her sense of self-worth, the old woman was more responsive to therapy. She even helped Kayla get tenure at the Institute.

Another year rolled by, and spring was in the air; but this year Charlene did not have an episode, although the nurses still attested that she had a sour disposition. One breezy April morning, Charlene and one of the nurses tapped on Dr. Harris's door. Charlene wanted to go outside for their morning talk. They strolled along quietly at first, then, when the nurse left them alone, Kayla initiated a casual conversation.

"The reports from your group session say that you have been interacting."

"The sprites think I'm their mother. I am no one's mother."

"Dr. Gupta says you have a positive affect on them, Charlene. And you are someone's mother. But I'm thrilled with the progress you've made. Dr. Stephens has even commented about you." Charlene tensed slightly at the mention of the head doctor.

"I know you don't like him much, He can be a hard pill to swallow. That and he is another man controlling you life. However, I believe that your distrust of the opposite sex will fade with time," Kayla said. "Just think to yourself, 'the man in front of me is not my husband. This person deserves a chance.'"

Charlene took a deep breath. "It wasn't so upsetting that he left me or took my money. It hurt that he took my children from me. I gave him everything and he left, just because he could. I raised my children with love for thirteen years, but some how that insane man, poisoned their minds in one week. That's why I cracked."

Kayla waited silently for Charlene to continue.

"I have kept you long enough," the old woman said. "The reason I asked you out here is not to rant about life. I want to leave."

"Are you sure you're ready?"

"No, but I don't need to be here any longer. Perhaps it's time I made a phone call or two."

"Who will you call?"

"God, first of all, and I'll thank Him for sending you to me. Then a call to someone who was once good to me."

"Charlene, I think you just said something nice."

Charlene rose from the bench without another word. Kayla barely stifled a chuckle as she watched her patient being ushered back to her room.

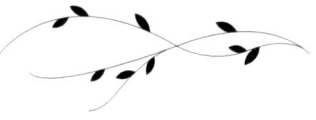

Charlene requested an appointment with Dr. Stephens to discuss her status at Hardaway Institute.

"Well, Mrs. Brighton," the head doctor said, "I see no reason why you should not be able to rejoin society.

You checked yourself in and can check yourself out. I trust you have some place to return to?"

"Yes, Dr. Stephens, I do. And please call me by my maiden name."

"Well, it seems to me you have been working on this for some time. However, I am going to have to ask that you seek regular counseling outside."

"Of course. Doctor, am I excused?"

"Yes. Good day, Ms. Georges."

Charlene walked out slowly, almost unsure of her footing. The uncertainty of what lay ahead suddenly felt heavy. She had made her phone calls, the second harder than the first. She was both surprised and relieved when Robert Funderburke answered her call. Robert had been her closest friend. Now she needed him again, and, sure enough, he had made arrangements for her to have a job and a place to live. Charlene was moving to a place she had thought she would never see again. She was starting over in the same place where her journey had begun.

> Dear Kayla,
>
> First I would like to apologize for not saying farewell in person. I don't want to say goodbye to you, I know we are not friends. That is unrealistic. You were doing your job, and for that I am grateful. Besides, Dr. Stephens wants me to seek out another counselor, so you will probably

receive reports soon. I promise to keep them interesting.

If you would like to contact me, the address is enclosed, along with a copy of my new manuscript. I hope you can read it to those sprites. They might enjoy it.

Sincerely,

Charlene A. Georges

Bend

I can't believe that I am on a rooftop. It's cold, windy, and I am on a rooftop. I can't believe I agreed to this. To be cold and super flexed in this position was not what I agreed to.

"Millie," Deshawn said, standing over her, holding her knees over her head, "you need to focus on breathing or you're going to pass out."

"Easy for you to say," she grunted.

"This is only a stretching position. I am doing all the hard work."

Millie grew quiet and tried to focus on what Deshawn had instructed her to do. *Breathe slowly in through the mouth and out of the nose. Focus only on the sound of your breathing. I should be in church on Sunday. Not on a roof breathing!*

Deshawn had been pestering her for weeks to let him get the stress knots out of her neck and shoulders. She had expected a massage, not yoga. She didn't know the first thing about yoga, only that it involved a lot of obscene posing. She was incredibly reluctant to allow Deshawn to do anything for her out side of the job. Even before she found out that he intended on put her through a grueling exercise session. He was an intern, after all, and being seen together outside the workplace would seem inappropriate. But the tension in her shoulders was getting worse, so she had finally given in to Deshawn's invitation. She thought back to their conversation a week ago.

"You carry a lot of unnecessary tension for someone who says their job is not brain surgery," he had said.

"Umm… You think I am tense?"

"Yes. Come *by* my apartment next Sunday—"

Millie cut him off. "I have church."

Deshawn took the last envelope to be mailed from her and gave her an unapologetic look. "God exists everywhere, in everything, and fellowship is not limited to a pew."

Deshawn's assertion had left Millie mildly unsettled. His statement was filled will rock-solid resolve, followed with a hint of irritation that he even had to say it. But Millie could not remember when she had not found her way to the Holy House (Millie's aunts call the church that, and she found herself saying it all these years later). She never proclaimed to be sanctified and holy. However she understood what it meant to have faith in the Lord, and be blessed. The thought Deshawn had presented her with was not foreign. She had heard people say it before, and to a degree she believed it herself. However, she could not justify not going to Service.

But then, when she woke up this morning and looked at her pressed suit, she did not want to put it on. A quiet voice whispered in her ear, *See something different.* Normally, she would say, "The devil is a lair," and go on her way, but her spirit was not conflicted and this seemed all right. So Millie quietly said a prayer, read her scripture of the day, and got ready the leave. The drive to Deshawn's apartment didn't take long, but the minute she knocked on his door, she got nervous. She had not called ahead. She thought about turning around. There was still time for her to get back to her normal routine. Before she could turn around, the door opened.

Deshawn was pleasantly surprised when he saw Millie standing on his doorstep. He pulled her inside and had her seated at his kitchen table before she could say anything.

"You look cold," he said. "I have some tea."

Tea together started out fine. Nice casual conversation, nothing out of the ordinary, until Deshawn grabbed her wrist and started bending and moving it. Millie was perplexed, and her face must have shown it, because when he looked at her again, he laughed heartily.

"Millie," he said, "you are going to have to relax and have an open mind if we are going to get through this morning.

Now, out on the roof and in an upside-down fetal position, she was wondering if this was supposed to be relaxing. The exercise proved that she was not totally inflexible in her old age, but it was not the most relaxing thing she had ever done. Deshawn was laughing at her so much she was beginning to think he had been plotting to embarrass her from the beginning. "I can't believe I let you talked me into this," she said. "Can you even do half the stuff you're making me do?"

"That and more. Sit up and observe."

As Millie watched, Deshawn sprang into action, moving in a fluid secession of poses. She suddenly felt jealous, a sentiment rooted in the fact that she never looked that contented and focused at the same time. After Deshawn's exhibition, they stayed on the roof a while longer and Millie finished the routine with fewer protests. By the time the noon sun started to warm the concrete garden, teacher, and student were winding down.

"You must be hungry," he said. "you should stay for lunch."

At first, Millie protested, but a gurgling in her stomach made her sit at the table. Deshawn gave her a wink and went into the kitchen, leaving her to explore the loft. The table she sat at was nestled between the kitchen and the stairs that led to the bedroom over her head. To her left was the living area, which had gone unnoticed until now, hidden behind the bookcase and the secretary beside the door. "I hope you're not getting bored at the office," she said, taking in the sweeping view of the city from his living room windows.

"No," he replied. "I just didn't realize how much correspondence went into a publication. To be honest, I started this internship just so I could get the extra nod for when I entered the broadcasting field."

"Is that so? Hey, where did you get all these masks?"

"My girl is in Africa. She sends a mask home occasionally. I'm house-sitting until she makes an honest man out of me." Pulling utensils out of drawers, he looked over his shoulder and saw Millie staring out the window.

"Would you believe that five years ago, this whole neighborhood was a slum?" he said. "Gentrification has worked wonders for this place."

"I heard about it on the news," Millie replied, "but I didn't really believe it. I don't frequent this side of town." He set their drinks and lunch on the table.

"I thought you would be health nut after this morning," she said giving their spread a critical look.

"Nope, I believe in moderation. Would you believe I used to smoke? Two packs of Newports a day. But Valeria didn't like it. I quit cold turkey after a year with her."

"What is she doing in the Motherland?"

Deshawn swallowed hard. "She is on her way to becoming a doctor. But, that is on hold no thanks to the influence of her old roommate. You know the type, ponytail wearing, artsy, and out there. Anyway she decided to join the Peace Corps. for a year before doing her residency. Now she is in West Africa somewhere, building wells and teaching kids to read."

"She's doing good work. Why didn't you go? That kind of work would have gotten you a nod, too." Millie pushed away memories of her younger self, and focused on the conversation about her host and his woman.

"I did go, for a week. I couldn't handle it. Then Katrina hit. It was easier for me to help bury the dead here than to see the look on some of those kids' faces."

"On the news, they always seem really hurt or really happy."

"That's just it. They live ten times worse than kids living in the ghetto here. And they still have hope. It was too damn eerie."

"Deshawn, sometimes I forget that you have so much experience. At thirty, all I did was move here and started my job."

"That is not a bad thing," he said between bites of his sandwich.

"No, it's not. But every now and again, I meet people who make me feel like I haven't done anything with my life," she admitted quietly.

"You just need to relax," he said. "The world is an interesting place to be experienced. But that doesn't mean everyone is supposed to explore it."

Millie pointed her fork at him accusingly. "Thanks for the words of wisdom, great sage." She smiled.

Deshawn shock his head. "It's all Val's bad influence."

"You miss her?"

"Yeah, but I guess I'll have to make do with you until she gets back."

He was too busy with his lunch to notice that Millie's eyes had grown as big as saucers and she had stopped breathing. Only when he asked her another question that went unanswered did he look up again. He laughed at her expression. "Millie, breathe! I was joking."

"What you said was inappropriate."

"I wish I had a camera out." He continued to chuckle. "That face is priceless."

"It isn't funny."

"See? You need to loosen up. Just be glad I'm not like I was in my heyday. A woman like you…. Well, let's just I was the use 'em and lose 'em type."

Millie stared blankly at the mask on the wall behind his head. "You remind me of a conversation I overheard in my favorite restaurant," she finally said. "Two young men walked in, they were the metro sexual type, so I dismissed them as family and continued eating. But at some point during their conversation, I began to listen to what they were saying. They weren't family, turns out that one was a man of faith and the other a shrewd businessman. The man of faith was having problems with his personal … well, his love life. It sounded like he was in love with one woman, but he just couldn't seem to avoid cheating on her. Even though he knew it was wrong. He said that it was childish, that at his age he ought to know better, but couldn't seem to stop himself. He sounded sincerely apologetic about hurting the woman that had his heart. The businessman seemed to know the couple very well. He never took sides. He just laid it on the line. And I want to say that he said something like," she paused to remember, "'well, you commit yourself to a lot of things in your life, like your work and Church, but it's hard to commit to a person because you can't predict what that person will say or do during the course of your relationship, that's why you have issues'. Their conservation went on about a number of things that I don't really remember what. By the time they left, I had developed a new respect for the modern brother. And I guess you remind me of them. You're at the point in your relationship that that dude was trying to reach."

Deshawn grinned from ear to ear." I sure never figured you for a romantic," he said. "You're just not used to seeing a role reversal. I, the man, am waiting for my woman to return from her dangerous trip of enlightenment, instead of it being the other way around. There is nothing profound about me and Valeria's relationship."

Not knowing how else to respond, Millie shrugged. Maybe Deshawn had a point. Maybe she did need to loosen up. But the question was how much, and did that mean more rooftop sessions? And if it did, would she be able to endure the throbbing of her sore muscles?

Winter break had just started. Deshawn was looking forward to the holidays. Valeria had phoned to say she was coming home with a big surprise. Thankfully, Millie had assured him that work would stop from the week before Christmas until the second of January; unfortunately, that meant she would work him to death as they pushed to get ahead before the New Year. Shaking the snow from his boots and dusting his head, Deshawn started up the stairs to the editing department.

He thought back to the first time he heard about this publishing house. Thunder Press was fairly new. It focused on new and local authors. He had been interviewed by Robert Funderburke, the man who had started the press with a few hand picked employees. In the beginning, Deshawn had actually hoped to shadow Funderburke, but the publisher had other ideas and sent him off to the Millie—and the wicked witch—with a smile.

For what it was worth, it wasn't as bad as he'd thought it would be. Every week was a different project, and there was also one constant assignment. At the beginning and end of each day, Deshawn would have to deal with Millie's "electrical correspondence," as she put it. The woman's apprehension towards the Internet amused him. She was also fun to watch (with Tanya on the sidelines) when she had a conniption when her schedule got thrown off. Then she turned into a juggernaut to correct the situation. If Deshawn had to describe her to anyone, he would sound like he was giving a professional referral: Millie is well spoken, well educated, and career-orientated. She likes everything in its proper place. She is also very analytical, a classic A type personality. These were the qualities that allowed her to excel as an editor. She has all the charm and wit to keep clients and employers happy. Side note: the idea of being carefree is as foreign to her as riding a camel down the main street of her hometown. That last thought made him snicker all the way up the stairs.

He hung his coat and scarf on the rack and waved at Tanya. Then Robert and Charlene emerged from her office, with a jovial air. When Charlene released they had an audience she immediately frowned. "Tanya," Robert crooned, "what a lovely sight you are this morning. How are you?"

Then he noticed Deshawn. "It is good to see you, too, Deshawn." Deshawn returned his greeting as Tanya gave him a mile-wide smile. "Where's Millie?" Robert asked. "She's usually here by now."

"She just called," Tanya said. "The traffic is really bad on her side of town."

"Fact of life; People freak out when there's moisture on the road. Anyway, I came to remind everyone of the holiday schedule and to announce that this year we will have a New Year's party." The publisher turned to Tanya. "Here are the event plans," he said. "Please make sure that our non-in-house people and these clients get a copy. Alright, then," he flashed another smile at his employees, "that's all I had to say this morning. I'll be in my office if you need me." He disappeared upstairs.

Deshawn had learned his lesson about Charlene early on. He darted into Millie's office, to avoid her. When he looked up to see if the mean lady had gone her way, he saw Tanya giving her a present wrapped in bright green paper and tied with a yellow bow. He was spying, and he knew it none of his business. But watching Charlene's face change as she pulled away the bow was, in a word, unbelievable. He didn't think the woman was capable of looking happy. She even smiled at Tanya, and that was definitely something remarkable. This smile wasn't that haughty smile she normally gave to everyone. This smile was soft and genuine.

Deshawn put all his thoughts about Charlene aside and set about his morning objectives. He pulled out the reference books and started taking notes that would be passed on to one of Millie's clients. However, after a few moments, he felt uncomfortable. He moved from his chair to Millie's desk. But, he was still uncomfortable. Putting his pen down, Deshawn stood up in the middle of the room and spun around. After five minutes of spinning around he still could not decide what was making him uncomfortable. But time was slipping by and he needed to finish up his assignment.

Millie arrived an hour later. By the time she walked into the foyer, it had stopped snowing. Now that she had made it to work safety, Tanya gave her the messages and Deshawn stopped fidgeting. *Maybe, I was just worried, he said to himself, or is it because I didn't think to get Millie something for Christmas.*

After the New Year's party, Deshawn decided to rearrange Millie's office as a present. The room needed better flow; a little feng shui would help. Or so Valeria suggested. It would be a more valuable gift than some trinket. He talked it over with Tanya during their lunch break. She thought it was a fun idea and agreed to help. As they moved things around, Tanya was very excited about moving one item in particular. It was the oversized box Millie had stored in the corner months ago. When they pulled the box out of the corner, Deshawn and Tanya were surprised to find a painting inside. After they hung it they ended up standing before it, stupefied.

"What are you two up to?" Millie's voice came from behind them.

"Millie," Tanya asked, "when did you have a portrait commissioned?"

Millie couldn't do anything but gape and shake her head. "I didn't model for this," she said.

Unable to read her body language, Deshawn asked, "Millie, are you upset that we changed the office around? We can put it back."

Tanya was still looking at the painting. "But that's you, right? Why would some random person just paint you ... like that?"

Millie looked around the room, anxiously searching for the packaging. Clutching the remnants of the box, she stuttered, "Tipinianca.... T... P... Taylar P. Nianca!" She looked like she was going to faint.

Deshawn rolled a chair out for her. "Are you sure it's from this Nianca person?" he asked.

"Yes, I'm sure. I recognize the style. I saw an exhibition of artists calling themselves *Les peintures révolutionnaires*. They toured ten cities doing different projects. They came to Savannah, with the Intimacy Project. Twelve artists presenting twelve paintings of the things their model considered an intimate gesture. And twelve images of things they didn't think were intimate."

"Only the French would think up a traveling porn show," Tanya snorted.

Millie laughed. "Sex is a child's idea of intimacy. Does Taylar's portrait of me have anything to do with sex?"

Deshawn looked more closely at the portrait. "No," he said, "but it looks like *Taylar* knew or saw a side of you we don't know about. But still ... why are you so upset?"

"So who is this, Taylar?" Tanya asked. "He's your ex-boyfriend, huh?"

Millie's starry eyed daze baffled and worried her co workers. "Ex-boyfriend? Former Mistress? Friend? Teacher? Artist? Explorer? Taylar is not easy to describe. Taylar is Taylar."

"So what does that make Taylar to you?" Deshawn asked.

Millie turned to him. "At first, Taylar was just another subject for the campus paper. But in two days, eleven hours, twenty minutes, and sixteen seconds, I fell in love. And then Taylar was gone. The group didn't know where their partner went. However they did have Taylar's pieces for the next four cities" She looked at the painting longingly before turning away again. "They let me see the rest of the collection. It's amazing what people let you get away with when they think they have an angry black woman on their hands. I memorized every brush stroke. This portrait was not among them. Truth be told, I was angry for a long time. All because I forgot the first thing Taylar told me. 'If you can trust, you can love. That's the path to true intimacy. Therefore, when you trust, do so wholeheartedly, and if that trust becomes love; accept it for everything it is worth, even it lasts for only a moment.' I got over it. Then I didn't care about or think about Taylar Nianca again. But right now, for some strange reason, I want to cry."

"Wow," said Tanya, "that's deep."

No one noticed Charlene standing in the doorway, listening. She stepped forward. "Millie, I am going to nominate you to be the travel writer for the new magazine. It is time you expanded your horizons."

"Where did you come from, Charlene?" Millie asked.

"You've become a little lackluster, Millie. You need to get out of this box for a while."

"But, Charlene," Tanya said, "she has to go through reviews and the portfolio…."

"I am aware of that, Tanya. I am also going see about getting Mr. Clemons a spot on staff when he completes his degree. He can move on when he loses his luster. In the meantime, Millie, you should start packing."

In Search Of

It had not occurred to me that it's been so long, and yet I remember every second. Every second I was in your presence.

A shower had become a rainstorm, flooding some distant back-alley art district. Here the beatniks and bohemians still met, alongside the techno geeks and aging entrepreneurs. Through the dense veil of falling water, the soft glow of an open café lit the street. There was a party in one of the upper flats. Music floated down, barely audible over the downpour. This was no tourist trap. No real tourists ever came here. It was too foreign, too far off the beaten path. Only the locals come here, and if you could blend in, you are more than welcomed.

Why am I still looking? That person is laughing at me, I know. 'Our emotions transcend time and space, and the receiver should get the message, just like e-mail.' If that's true, then that person is definitely laughing.

Standing under a lone streetlight, a figure wrapped in a wet trench coat was checking soggy directions. The evening had begun with a cool refreshing shower, which was followed by this nighttime squall. The directions give little information, so the reader stuffs them away without hesitation.

All these years, and not a word, not a smoke signal, nothing. Then one day out of the blue … you… you just reenter my life. You would say, 'Our emotions are intangible. It's the memory from which our emotions stem that makes those feelings meaningful.' Philosophical nonsense! I am tired of grasping at memories! I need to know it was real.

This place was like a hundred others. The globe could be condensed into back alleys like this one. Everything that can be bought or experienced transpires in places like this. The café was starting to close allowing the darkness of night to seep out of the margins. The streetlamp felt like the sun, a lone beacon against the void. Its light neutralizing the black holes produced by enormous puddles.

The trench coat moved on in aimless abandon. The end of the road came in the blink of an eye. Three streets over, the beaten path was in plain sight, but there were no treasures over there, only trinkets for those who would mistake the falling rain for falling stars. There was a distant flicker in the void, a forgotten star, a lonely twinkle that beckoned the Seeker away from complacent mediocrity.

Our time together seemed so wondrous, almost infinite. We were in search of grand aspirations in those youthful days; I wonder if you found everything you wanted. My path wants to entwine with yours. Perhaps, I have become needy, or selfish to hunt for you this way.

The trench coat traveled the path to that faint star. Its window was large enough for mannequins garbed in strange costumes to parade among crafts and photographs. Then there it was, found in the moment when all hope was lost. But the light was fading. It was still raining and time was slipping away. The door was tried. It was locked. The Seeker began to bang on the door in desperation, shouting in four languages, hoping that one of them would be heard and understood.

Divine intervention turned the lights back on. An older man came to the door with an irate look on his face. His solicitor pointed and pled with elated hope and the fear of disappointment. The owner scarcely cared that the plane was leaving in the morning, didn't care that the directions had not been clear, that the search had taken ages. But through the chatter, he could hear clearly. "I know the artist." The old man unlocked the door. He was saluted like a king for his trouble.

The owner motioned to his guest to sit and locked his door again. The rain was subsiding. The world was slowing down. The owner listened to the story in its entirety. He brought the painting forward and placed it on an easel to be examined. The owner said he didn't know its origin, but that its title was *Ayala*. His guest smiled. There were tears of joy.

After so long, I've found something of you?

The owner prepped his register. The guest gave him two cards: one plastic, one with an address. The guest thanked the owner one last time. Tears rolled against a broadening smile. The door had a little bell whose soft jingle had been nullified by the noise of the storm. The bell had a pleasant jingle. The kind of sound that should awaken someone from a dream. The storm gave way to the bright moon, heralding the end of this journey.

Arrangements

Aisha sat in her favorite coffee shop for her lunch break. She by the window reanalyzing the plans she has implemented since the morning she destroyed her kennel.

It's messed up. How did it come to this, I was so close. Damn that Baja. But at least he sent some cronies to get the lot cleared out. It's better this way. Now I got to go tell Ms Elly that we—I mean, she is going to rent out her house to the youth ministries. It will be the chaps' piece of the country near the city. The landscaper did a great job. It looks like a park back there. I am a bad, bad girl, hiding my sins behind a senile old lady and the church. Well, Mr. Gibson, you got me out of another one. Your funeral put me in contact with a lot of useful folks. I am definitely going to burn for this.

Ms Elly won't mind too much. She's in a nice nursing home and I've seen to it that all her finances are taken care of. When poor Miss Elly took to wandering and forgetting things, I couldn't leave her alone in that big house. She likes Rolling Green, and the staff is on point. That good-for-nothing ex of mine getting locked up for ten to twenty was one of the highlights of my life. The situation just gives me more time with my surrogate mom. I always liked visiting Ms Elly. As far as she's concerned, I can do no wrong. My own mom was always spit and nails with me, but with Ms. Elly, it was always, 'Aisha, baby, you want honey on ya biscuits?' I miss when she'd make them just for me, even after me and that fool split up. If Rodney had watched his back, Ms. Elly wouldn't have had to call me. 'Aisha, baby, Rodney in trouble and done left me here wit dem dogs. And dese boys been callin' to da house looking for em.' Luckily, I know most of those jokers, and Baja knew Patches, and next thing I know, I am dealing in puppies.

Anyway, it's time I close that chapter. But I have to admit that this final smoke screen to throw off the feds might be a bit much. Taking on a roommate, is a little extreme. I even skipped some monthly bills, just to make it look like I'm struggling. I got rid of the prepaid phone, so no worries there. Watching spy movies came in handy. I think that is every thing. I built Doris and Shell a kennel in the backyard. I'll just have to take them to a park. I need to … Wait a minute. Is that who I think it is?

Aisha watched in disbelief as the man she did not want to see again, emerge from a parked van. He jogged across the street and into the coffee shop. She continued watching the parking lot in hopes that the appearance of the agent had nothing to do with her. Unfortunately, that hope was dashed when a familiar form slid into the seat across from her.

"You never called," he said with a hint of mischief. The play in his voice almost made Aisha think she had jumped the gun. *Maybe he isn't a fed.* But she dismissed the thought. She trusted her instincts.

"I am sorry?" she replied.

"I was waiting."

She shrugged. "Not my problem. I don't even know you. Why should I call you?"

He stuck out a hand. "Ulysses Kingsley, but most call me U.K. Now can we get down to business?"

"You got to be kidding." Ignoring the hand, she got up to leave. Before she was out of ear shot she heard him reply.

"I'll be seeing you."

Ulysses leaned back to watch Aisha leave. As he enjoyed the view of her swaying hips, his Bluetooth buzzed.

"Why are you following her? You're not even supposed to be out in the open."

"The view is lovely. Besides, doing something like that won't do us any good."

"She's the reason all the targets have gone to ground. Someone else can bring her in for questioning"

"Relax." Ulysses grinned into his coffee cup. "There is a better way to do what needs doing. They'll resurface, but in the meantime, let me worry about the lady."

"You're lucky you have not been shipped back to Tennessee."

Ulysses ended the call, and sank in to the chair. His wasn't about to let the chain of command stress him out. The handlers were impeding his hunt, with all their unnecessary restrictions. He had the investigation under control, despite this minor hang up.

Aisha hurried back to her office. Revising and uploading her ad for a roommate had just moved up to priority one. The first line read, "Must love dogs."

The following weeks were a blur of faces and names. In addition to her inability to choose a roommate, she also had to endure the stress of her mother's nagging. She encountered argument after argument. Her mother insisted that she would be giving up her precious privacy, and that if she wanted a roommate so bad, she should move back home. And if Ms. Shirley had not run that in ground, she said that it was just foolish, more times than Aisha could count. Telling Mom the truth behind her actions was out of questions, so Aisha maintained a simple defense: she could pay off the house faster with the extra money. Besides, she had two over-protective guard dogs, so her security would not be a question. After a lot of bickering and fussing, her mother finally gave up and decided to ignore her daughter's latest fiasco.

Six weeks later, Aisha took one more application. The applicant sent a fax containing references, a copy of credit history, and a list of questions. Aisha instantly liked this one. She phoned Ms. Johnson immediately. Three days later, Millie met with Aisha at her favorite coffee shop. They were well suited for each other.

The Magazine was stationed in the North Carolina. A place Millie did never expected to live. And not knowing how long she would be there didn't want to rush into buying a new home. When she learned about Aisha's rental space it seemed like the perfect compromise. She would not have all the added responsibilities of owning property; while dealing with the stresses of being a transplant resident and adjusting to a new work environment. Living with another working professional, was just what she needed.

They had the same conclusions about each other as the interview progressed. They approached the situation like the Camp David Accord, in order to maintain each other autonomy. Two mocha lattes later, Aisha was driving home with a passenger. Inside the house, they were greeted by Doris, who gave Millie a warning growl, while Shell remained curled up in his bed. Aisha quickly intervened and the let Doris meet Millie, who cautiously let the huge dog sniff her hand and decide if they were going to be friends or not. Aisha watched hopefully. Two other candidates had been scared off by Doris's size. But Millie did not appear to be intimidated. "Doris," she said, petting the animal, "be nice to this prospective roommate." Soon enough, Doris snorted and lumbered off to retrieve her chew toy.

Millie smiled "She's friendly. Can we continue the tour?"

"Sure. There's a gourmet kitchen and formal dinning room down the hall on the left. The dogs are not allowed in there. The washer and dryer are under the stairs. We will only share this floor."

"The den seems bare. Do you mind if I put my media stuff in there?"

"No, but I usually put Doris and Shell in there at night."

"They aren't going to hump on my couch, are they?"

"No. Shell is neutered, and Doris goes outside during that time. Do you want to see the mother –in-law suite now?" When Millie nodded, Aisha led her through the kitchen to a door leading to the ground level garage.

Millie's suite was a good size for someone starting over. She had a bedroom, a closet, a bathroom, and some open space. Sharing the kitchen would be fine, and she had somewhere to watch her movies. The house was a contemporary cookie cutter with too much space for one person. Millie was sold.

Millie and Aisha agreed on three-month trial to see how things worked out. Much to Aisha's pleasant surprise, Millie was like a shadow. Although Aisha saw evidence of the other woman's presence in the home, Millie was rarely physically present. The den became a very comfortable media room, thanks to the renter, not that she was ever around to use it. Millie had assignments that kept her away most of the time. One of the signs that she had returned was that the kitchen was stocked with health-nut foods. Organic, was not a common term in Aisha's grocery vocabulary, but she had to admit some the stuff was pretty tasty. Other than that, she felt she had definitely hit the renter lotto. Or so she thought.

Millie started receiving a lot of packages. Not the small As-Seen-On-TV boxes, or the subscription kind of boxes, but huge packages with *fragile* stamped all over them. Aisha did some mild investigating to make sure these boxes would not bring trouble back into her life. Much to her relief, what Millie received was quite benign.

Aisha's fears set aside; she continued the search to find her prize bitch a mate.

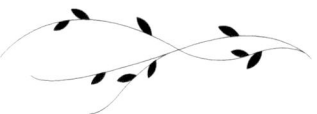

Despite Aisha's careful planning and caution, she could not keep the lustful eyes of Ulysses from wandering her way. Four months later, on Labor Day weekend, he appeared again. Aisha had decided to take Shell and Doris to the park for some quality time. Even dogs need extra attention sometimes. They ran around, chasing balls and barking, and Aisha was so wrapped up in playtime that she didn't notice the watcher on the park bench. Any passerby would not think twice about the watcher. He was nothing out of the ordinary, with his dog sitting beside him as he shelled and ate peanuts. That was the impression an average person might have, but the person approaching him was not average.

"Hey, mind if I take a load off?"

Ulysses turned to the intruder. He had noticed the dude's approach from the other side of the park. The view told him that something was up. This was not an everyday cat. Sure, he was Roca-clad and had the swagger, but everything about said he was not average. Ulysses matched him in height, but pound for pound, it was more like Lewis vs. Jones. That aside, he nodded the okay for the stranger to have a seat.

"Nice weather," the stranger ventured. "The view is nice, too."

This guy is a chatty bugger, probably a fairy. Ulysses just nodded and kept one eye on Aisha and the other on the stranger.

"You more interested in the dogs or the woman?" the stranger asked.

Ulysses turned his head slowly. "What's it to you?"

The stranger smirked, stood up, and approached the preoccupied Aisha. When he got too close, however, Doris reared up, growling to let her mistress know that they had company.

Aisha was ecstatic to see her cousin. "Patches! When did you get back?"

"Yesterday. Do you know you have eyes on you?"

Straining to look over his shoulder as they hugged, Aisha sighed. She was hoping she had just been imagining things. But to her annoyance the scowling fed still had his eyes latched on them. "Yeah," she said. "It's a fed."

Patches held her at arms' length, a stern look on his face. "I told you to stay out of trouble while I was gone."

Aisha shrugged him off. "It's alright. They got nothing on me. That one's just sniffing."

Patches grinned. "I thought as much. You should invite him to the cookout. I doubt he's on the clock. I didn't notice any characters on the way in." This earned him a punch in the shoulder.

"Are you mad!?"

"Maybe, besides, it's that or I deck him for stalking my cousin, and there goes my career in the military"

"You wouldn't."

"The guy was staring a hole in your ass. Hell, yeah, I'd lay him out. He's staring hard, am I right?"

Patches stood with his back to Ulysses, using his broad shoulders to shield Aisha. Not that he needed to shield Aisha from anything. He had made sure while they were growing up that she could take of herself when he wasn't around. The problem was that Aisha liked to get in the *midst*, as she put it, and wind up in a whole lot of mess. Patches would always have her back, but with the feds involved, he was not sure if he could bail her out.

Aisha craned her neck to look around him. It was just as Patches thought. U.K. had not taken his eyes off them. She only snorted a confirmation.

"Well?" her cousin asked.

"Well what?"

"What are you going to do?"

Aisha rolled her eyes. She had done everything she could think to come off the radar for indictment. That meant there was only one thing left to do: stop acting like a suspect and act like an average woman. Leashing her pets, she gave Patch an apathetic look. "Guess I'll have to give him a taste. How did you find me, anyway?"

"Your roommate told me. She's cute. Where'd you find her?"

"I don't think you want to go there. Come on. Let's go visiting."

Without giving Ulysses another look, Aisha loaded her babies into the DeVille. She would deal with him later. She truly hoped he would just go way, but someone had once told her once you're on fedar (federal radar), you stay on fedar, maybe for years. She had nothing to hide anymore, but still, she didn't want them following her everywhere she went. Especially not at the family cookout, the safe haven where she could relax with her cousins and let the dogs lumber about.

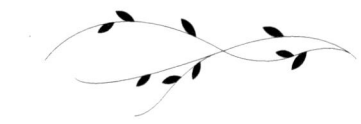

The cookout was great, better than a planned reunion. Patches, Aisha and some other cousins went off into the woods to have a smoke and mingle. Aisha didn't do much of either. She sat on a fallen tree and stared at *his* card and her cell phone. If she called, it could just be walking into an elaborate setup. Or she'd have a permanent stalker on her hands. If she didn't call, she would never know. The smart thing to do would be to call the police. Let them handle it. The reckless thing to do would be to hit Send. The smart thing was being pushed aside by the reckless thing. That once-a-month itch was creeping up fast, and she would have to call somebody sooner or later. The usual emergency dick was getting boring, and a toy was out of the question, which only left the mole. What was life about if not to take a risk? She hit Send.

The phone rang and rang and she was about to hang up when the voice mail picked up. That smooth accent touched a sensitive nerve. "Make the message brief," it said. "I am a busy man."

The arrogance, but that's what I like. The beep sounded. "Book a room, someplace nice. I'll meet you there."

When she closed the phone, she found herself in a headlock. "So you think you can play with the big boys, eh?"

"Get off me, Patches. I'm grown, I can handle myself."

"Come on, Job is telling one his stories." Patches pulled her off the log and into the family.

Meanwhile, Ulysses was sitting in a sports bar waiting for his contact. Despite the noise from the ball game, he heard his phone. But he did not answer it, thinking that the recorded message might be more useful. As always, his contact was taking his sweet time, but after a haphazard report, and a reprimand, it would be over and he could get back to work. Keeping tabs on Aisha was not just recreation. She was obviously connected, and chances were that she would lead to someone else. He looked at his phone to find out who was calling. It was a local number. Even better, it was Miss Harris's number. He had replayed the message for a fifth time when his contact finally pulled up a stool.

"What's the score, my friend?"

Ulysses did not bother with the usual cryptic talk. He had devised a plan wherein he could have his cake and eat it, too. "You remember that hungry kid, Neal? Sell those dogs to him; tell him I'm breeding a fresh pair. If we play it right, this one is going to be our golden ticket. One more thing—if that kid is still working security at the Omni, get me a room there, the same night he is on."

"That place is pricey."

"Call me when it's set up." Ulysses finished his drink and left the contact sitting at the bar.

Much to the dismay of his current handlers, Ulysses did not believe in timetables. He had gotten this assignment because he understood dogs. When it came to man or beast, he had one philosophy: a lot of time, patience, and work had to be invested before either could be used. Tenure as a detective plus two generations of K-9 unit veterans had taught him that. He had been working on a murder case in Tennessee when the suspects started crossing state lines and the evidence was leading to other criminals and crimes. The Bureau got involved not long after the first bust. They had their eye on Bartholomew Jackson, also known as Baja, for trafficking, illegal gambling, and animal endangerment. It only made sense for them to recruit Ulysses. He was already under, and all he had to do was go a little deeper.

Ulysses had calculated his way through all of Baja's contacts, getting introduced to one middle man after another until he met The Man. All he needed to close the case was to catch Baja in the act of doing anything illegal. His sole miscalculation was meeting Aisha Harris. Her name was not unfamiliar to him. She had been briefly mentioned by their snitch, Rodney Watson, who turned out be her former lover. Watson insisted that she had nothing to do with business, but that was probably before he got busted. In reality Aisha was neck deep in it. She'd become connected with all sorts of people, to further her experiment. That is how she got wind of his dogs. According to Baja, she was worth meeting, even if what she wanted would seem unusual. But Ulysses had taken her too lightly and messed up.

One call is all it took, and out the window went the whole case. All the targets had gone ghost, leaving the team with nothing, not even a rumor. By the time Ulysses put it together that Harris was at the cause, she had covered her tracks. Her kennel was gone, her records probably destroyed. Only the house was left, with a paper trail leading back to Ms. Elly Watson; the mother of Rodney Watson. On the surface it looked like Aisha was simply taking care of her ex-boyfriend's senile mother. Aisha's financial records revealed that she was like many other Americans, living above her means and in debt. Ulysses on the other hand, found Miss. Harris to be calculated and cunning, and did not believe that the data was telling the whole story. He made it clear to the handlers that if one call was all it took undo all their hard than another one might redeem them. Therefore he was going to make it his personal mission to use his time with Miss Harris more wisely, the second time around.

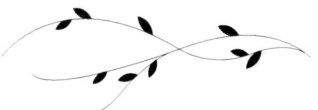

To Aisha's dismay, the weekend ended uneventfully, and by Wednesday she was pretending that she didn't care if the phone rang or not. She wanted the phone to ring very badly. The waiting only made her angry and more suspicious. Something was not right. What man (federal agent or not) turns down a good lay, especially when she's the lay?

She took an early lunch, while nursing coffee in the break her cell phone rang. Fumbling to get it out of her purse, she was slightly deflated to see it was just a text message. She would have preferred to hear a rich baritone, but all she got was a black and white message. She read the message with a smirk, and a growing anticipation of wearing the pink teddy hiding in her dresser.

It seemed like an eternity before the week came to an end and she could get her itch scratched. She was hot and bothered long before she snapped the last clasp of her garter belt on the lacey thigh-high stockings. She gave herself the once-over in the vanity mirror, pleased with the seductive image. A light dusting of make up enhanced her features. There was no sense in using a lot for it to get smeared everywhere. The 'do' is spiky and sassy, instead of hard spritzed curls. She applied a little more of her "*sugar daddy*" lip gloss. She wanted to not only smell like a walking piece of candy (thanks to her new bottle of *Envy Me*) but to taste like it, too. Sliding into her four-inch heels and pulling a three quarter length grey swing coat, she ushered her pups downstairs to their sitter.

Millie looked up from her notebook to acknowledge Aisha as Doris hunkered beneath the writer's feet to coax a belly rub. "You're just lucky my plans changed," she told Aisha. "Have fun, hot mama."

Aisha didn't pay the little jab any mind, she had it all worked out. Happily she tipped her way to the garage and slid into the DeVille. Turning over the ignition and hitting the lights, she was ready to begin the trek uptown. But before she could crest the portal, a sliver gleam caught her eye and she spotted the gray finish of the Suzuki 900 propped against the far wall. "That Millie is always full of surprises," she murmured as she backed out the drive to encounter her thrill ride for evening.

Forty minutes later, she pulled into the hotel's parking deck. The security guard could barely tell her how to get into the building, his grin was so wide. But she brushed him off and found her own way in. The lobby was classy, to say the least, and as she eyed the black marble and gold embellishments she was glad she paid taxes. But spending so much for a one-night stand in a place like this seemed a bit much, whether it was for information or a piece of ass. However, standing in the middle of the floor gaping was killing the high-class hooker look she was going for and replacing it with country bumpkin. *Not cute.* It would have been nice if Ulysses had shown up right then.

Brushing aside any mood-killing thoughts, she sauntered toward the reception desk and asked for Mr. Kingsley's room. Despite the clerk's snobby manner, they had a pleasant exchange that gained Aisha an envelope and the room key. She waited until she was alone in the elevator to read her note. Thirty seconds later, she wished she had not bothered to open it. It was an arrogant message from a conceited man. If he were anyone else, she would not have come. If she were not caught in the grip of the horrible monster called lust, she would not be half naked and randy with anticipation. But knowing she was playing with fire was making the experience irresistible. The elevator came to a halt on the twenty-second floor. She found Room 2257. As the plastic card slid into of the lock pad, her mind raced. What was she going to find inside?

The suite had a dim glow, but at least it was not black, beige, or gold; she'd seen enough of that in the lobby. This was a soothing flow of royal blue and vanilla, a calming contrast to the skyline showing through the windows. A bucket of champagne and chocolate dipped strawberries were the next items to catch her eye. Tossing her jacket aside, she poured herself a generous glass, and indulged in the candied fruit. Lazily scanning the horizon, she soon realized that the room could be easily watched from the office building across the street. Maybe she was being paranoid, but it was a logical conclusion. Toying with the blinds, she considered closing them, but decided that the idea of having an audience to this little tryst would be more fun. She left the blinds alone. If the feds wanted a performance, she would give them one.

Ulysses knew when Aisha entered the hotel. He saw her when she picked up the key. He had planned it all ahead of time. But he had to make sure that the right people saw her too. Ulysses had made contact with Neal early in the week. The kid was suspicious as expected, but Ulysses keeps the dialogue short and to the point. He put the bug in Neal's ear that he may be looking for a buyer in the near future. But after tonight the pawn would take the bait and run with it. That left one last task for the night. Miss Harris had essentially served her purpose, and he should walk away. Leaving the building without crossing the line, and keeping his professional code of ethics should had been his top priority. But he just couldn't keep himself from making mistakes when it came to that woman. He had watched her walk across the lobby, and he really liked the roll-bounce movement of her hips. He rubbed his hand over the beard he had not yet gotten used to, even after months of growing it.

Rubbing it had become a sign of his irritation. Indecision was keeping him in that lobby.

But he'd be damned if he passed up on the nymph waiting in his room. Ulysses pulled himself from the comfort of his observation station, and got on the same elevator that Aisha had ridden. The confined space was still full of the lingering scent of a woman's perfume. Ulysses entertained himself with the thought that it was hers. The smell with thick and sweet without being overpowering, it reminded him of candy. He got off on the twenty second floor and proceeded to door that match the room number. He banished any second thoughts. It was wrong, deliciously wrong. Not wanting to spook his guest, Ulysses opened the door cautiously. He had told his keepers that they did not need to send surveillance. But the damn perverts could not resist the prospect of watching a live porno, and set up shop anyway. Ulysses calmly resigned himself to the thought it was his civic duty to enter the overprice hotel room and fuck this woman into submission in the name of justice.

He waited a minute to allow his eyes to adjust to the darkness. The vision before him said there was nothing separating him from the prize, even though his instincts were saying something else: *You know she's wearing some kind of lingerie. And you, soldier boy, should touch every inch of lace, sateen, or silk that covers that very feminine form standing in the window before you rip it off and bend her over.*

The instant his hand touched the rise of her hip, Aisha leaned forward. As their body fit flush together, she gave him as slow and inviting grind.

"You ate all the strawberries," he teased her, tracing her back and shoulders with a finger.

"No, I didn't. I saved you the juiciest one. Are you ready for it?"

Ulysses had every right to have a smug look on his face. His bedmate still lay unconscious, exhausted and snoring, while he had showered and dressed. Only when the smell of fresh coffee filled the air did he notice a change in the sleeping woman. The rustling of sheets was followed by sharp groan, and Aisha's eyes flew open in response to the spasm of her overworked loins. Only able to flop onto her back, Aisha lay staring at the ceiling and collecting her thoughts.

Ulysses took the opportunity to seize and toy with one of her exposed nipples.

"Off!" She pushed him away. "I'm not ready yet."

The sight of her discomfort only heightened his machismo. "Too bad. I could go a few more rounds."

Aisha rolled her eyes. "Shut up. I hope your friends enjoyed the show."

"Friends?"

"Whatever." She tried to move, but the large hand on her chest prevented her from getting up.

"Stay," he said. "It'll be a while before housekeeping comes knocking."

"The government must pay well for you to afford to shack up in a place like this." She grinned as she threw out the cynical jab. But Ulysses quickly ended her prickly mood by suckling and licking her lips. "I don't know what you're talking about," he said. "I am just a man with expensive interests." He stood up, pulled his jacket on, and exited the room; leaving Aisha alone to deal with her aches and rekindled desire.

When Ulysses reached the lobby, his phone rang. The keepers were checking in. The plan was working. Neal had been standing behind the desk when Aisha arrived. The plan was working out just like Ulysses said it would. He could consider his romp with the breeder his reward.

Secret Lives

When Aisha came in from walking Shell and Doris, she was surprised to see her tenant in the living room, watching television.

"Hey!" she said, "I thought you were in Rio or something."

Millie waited for the woman and dogs to enter the room before replying. "No. I went to Roanoke to see the leaves change. It's beautiful this time of year."

Shell charged across the room to get petted as Millie idly flipped through the channels.

"Only you would drive through hick land," Aisha said.

"It's not that bad. Besides, I had backup. How do you feel about a movie night? I know it's against your code and everything, but I'd appreciate the company."

"It's not a code," Aisha said. "It's just good business sense. You don't have to be friends with the landlady. I haven't eaten yet. Do you feel like Chinese or pizza?"

"Landlady? I prefer to think of you as my neighbor. And pizza sounds good. I'll call the pizzeria."

When the pizza was on its way, Millie opened the entertainment unit and pulled a few DVDs out of their hodgepodge collection. Aisha called out a few titles and they settle on the odd lineup of Casablanca, *The Fences*, and Scarface.

"We need beer," Millie muttered, heading to the kitchen. By the time, she returned the first movie had started. She gave Aisha a bottle of *Michelob*. "I'm going on a long trip, coming up" she said.

"That's nothing new. What has you in a funk?"

"My family wants me to come home for the holidays, and I don't want to go."

Aisha gave her pointed look "You would rather go to the middle of nowhere than see your family?"

Millie nodded her head.

"Why?"

"You don't know my family. They're gonna ask a bunch of unnecessary questions, like, Why aren't you married? Are you going to a good church? Not one of those TV charlatans, I hope? Why did you give up your position and condo in exchange for a roommate and a job that has you gallivanting about like a hobo?"

Aisha couldn't help but laugh. "Sorry," she said. "Sorry. But doesn't every family ask those questions? Just give them some generic answers and move on."

"It's not that easy," Millie said. "I have two brothers … and then there's the feud…. It's like we're some Technicolor version of *Dynasty*. 'Aunt Jessie, she thinks she knows everything. My mom calls her the lying heifer.' And says, 'you know how your cousins are, we cannot have them over.' My Grandfather gets meaner every year, so you have to watch what you say or he might shot. He keeps a rifle around in case the Sheets show up." Both women were laughing by now. "And," Millie continued, "'will someone make sure Ida took her meds and keep Calvin out the liquor?' They were grooming him for politics until the accident. And here's my favorite. 'Howard (my brother the lawyer), tell us about all the important people you know.' What makes it worse is that my brother the lawyer married the mayor's daughter, the silly Barbie Doll that she is. It never ends. They're a bunch of snobs just because they own over a quarter of the land in that backwater town and the church was built by our maternal great great grandmother's second husband. And the only reason my dad's family owns the land is because great Uncle Roscoe Johnson blackmailed the sheriff. If it wasn't for the pulled pork and collard greens," she finished, "I wouldn't even consider going."

Aisha laughed herself into a bellyache. "That … that is… Wow… I have never heard you talk so much. Or sound so hostile."

"It's not funny! And to make matters worse, I have to deal with them on top of jet-lag."

"Millie, that's what trips me out about you. You're willing to go to the far ends of the earth for that magazine, but you won't drive six hours to visit your family. Just put on that dusty Casablanca coat of yours and go see your people!" Aisha finished her statement with a deep swig of beer to cool her throat.

"Why don't you come with me?" Millie asked. "There are a lot of natural tourist attractions there."

"You are not going to con me into visiting your people, and sightseeing isn't my thing. Besides, I have enough troubles with my own family."

Millie raised an eyebrow. "Do you? You don't talk about 'em." The beer was starting to get to her, and she was only able to focus on Aisha's busy hands. She watched as Aisha pulled a wooden box out under the couch. And out of the box came a small plastic baggie full of leaves, a box of rolling papers, matches, and a plastic container. Aisha twisted the container in half, and then carefully poured a portion of the green leaves and seeds into the bottom.

"What is that for?" Millie asked.

"This is a grinder. It crushes the seeds and makes the leaves finer for a smoother smoke." Aisha held up the cap up so Millie could see the plastic blades inside it. Then she demonstrated how the tool worked, twisting the two halves together, and grating the leaves and seeds into a fine mulch. She emptied the flakes onto a paper, made a fold and glided the long side along her tongue to seal the paper. Then using friction created by her hand on her thigh to roll it up in one quick motion. To Millie, it looked like poetry in motion, a skilled trick learned from years of practice. But when her landlady offered her the first puff she had to turn it down.

"A contact is good enough for me."

"More for me, then," Aisha said. "I don't talk about my family 'cause they're just my family. Mom, my aunts and uncles, my brother, we just share the same blood.

That's all we have in common. Only my cousin Patches and I are tight. Now that he's in the Marines, I don't get to see him that much."

Millie opened another beer. "Patches?"

"Don't tell me you been up North so long you forgot how we name our chaps in the dirty South"

"My family is uppity. Did you forget?"

"I gotcha. We were always in the midst as kids. But we grew up, got a little smarter. Patches … you can call him Patrick, he's a career Marine. He has been in for almost ten years now, Whoa Core and all that mess." She leaned back against the cushions, enjoying the inhale.

"Your family sounds normal to me."

"That's why I picked you, ya know. As long as it doesn't affect your little world, you don't care. We've been living in the same house for like the burning hour now, and this is the first time either of us has said more than hello and goodbye."

"I thought you wanted it that way."

"I'm not complaining. But haven't you ever wondered why I got a roommate?"

Millie sipped her beer, staring at the floor. Aisha's sudden interest in their living arrangement perplexed her. It had been only by chance that she had found out about Aisha's basement suite. An acquaintance of an acquaintance of Millie's secretary knows Aisha. It always amazed Millie how people affected each others' lives without knowing it. But why she was currently in Aisha's life she did not know, nor had she taken the time to examine this topic.

"No," she finally said. "Not really."

Taking another puff, Aisha gave Millie a weighty look. "Tell me why you're putting together a gallery in my basement, and I'll tell you why I needed a roommate like you."

"Why does it matter all of a sudden?"

"Beer and herb make me chatty."

Millie settled back and tried not to laugh at Aisha drug-induced commentary on the film they were sort of watching. When the door bell rang, Aisha jumped up, fumbling for money to pay the pizza boy. The bittersweet smell of the herb must have been strong, because the minute she made eye contact with him, he gave her a knowing wink and headed back to his tricked out Supra. When she returned to the den, only her two spoiled dogs where waiting. She gave the pair a treat of meat and cheese from the box before sentencing them upstairs for the night.

"Millie?" she called. When there was no answer, she assumed that her roommate had gone to the bathroom and resumed her smoking and drinking.

"You might understand if I show you." Millie's voice came from behind the sofa. She had come back into the room so quietly that Aisha hadn't noticed.

Aisha looked around, but Millie was already heading back to her part of the house. Bitten by the curiosity bug, Aisha followed her down the kitchen stairs to Millie's mini-storehouse of books, memorabilia, and art. The tour came to a stop in Millie's bedroom. At first, Aisha didn't get it. What she saw was just a portrait of a girl in a sheer white sundress, the shade and light of the paint revealing her form beneath the fabric. The girl was standing in a hallway, looking at some unseen object, perhaps a mirror. At first glance the pretty face in the picture looked sure and confident, but the eyes were innocent and amazed by what they were seeing. The girl was leaning away from the thing she encountered, betraying apprehension or fear. Overall, the painting revealed vulnerability. Aisha was taken aback by the sudden sense that she was spying on this girl, catching her in a moment confusion or uncertainty. It was a beautiful piece, in which the muted colors expressed a multitude of meanings and implications.

"So," Aisha finally said, "you like this person's work and buy the reproductions?"

"The girl is me, and most of these are Taylar's originals. The prints belong to random artists who remind me of Taylar. I gave up everything to find the one who painted my portrait," Millie confessed with mild embarrassment.

"Are you in love with this person, or something?"

"I don't know. I don't think so. How I feel about Taylar isn't easy to describe. Anyway it's your turn."

"I am sleeping with a federal agent who wants me to roll on the dog men."

Millie had not expected anything legally incriminating to fall out of Aisha's mouth. After a minute, she said, "He must not come with benefits if you need a roommate."

"I never thought I'd tell anyone what I was doing on the side, and that's all you have to say?"

"It's not my business. If someone asks me, all I can say is that Aisha is my landlady. We don't go any deeper than that." Millie gave a wink and a smile. A minute later, wanting to steer the conversation away from anything that might land them in the state penitentiary, she said, "So tell me, why is your cousin's name Patches?"

"I couldn't say Patrick when we were kids," Aisha explained, comforted by the thought that Millie's change of topic was a hint that she understood.

The next week could not have been better, for Aisha. Monday afternoon, an associate contacted Aisha about a dog that had been abandoned, one that exhibited all the key features she was looking for in a mate for Doris. After work, she high-tailed it to the country to have a look at this wonder dog. He was everything she had dreamed off, the perfect mate for her precious Doris, at least on the out side. She contacted her veterinarian the next morning to have the blood work done. His temperament was not exactly what she wanted, but it would do if the genetics matched up, the litter would be physically amazing. Although she truly believed in the genetic vigor of hybrids, she was painfully away that not every hybrid was equal. That's why a standard, with specific bred characteristics and lineage are necessities for man's best friend. Aisha believed she was on the verge of creating something lasting. It all started with Max and Megan, how she loved them. Megan was beautiful, blue grey, obedient and protective Cane corso. Max was a blue nose pit and a lilac Sharpei, a loyal laid back kind of dog.

Aisha loved their huge heads and strong bodies. She thought of them as perfect in every way. Max ironically was a gift from Rodney. Mad was supposed to be breed from fierce fight dogs. But he came out the runt of the litter and lacking aggressive tendencies.Rodney's friends were going cull him or worse. But,the fates must have on Max's side, because ended his days after a pampered life. It that cooper head had not gotten into the kennel and bitten him, she would still have Max. That dog was the only good gift Rodney gave her, that and a surrogate mother.

She was so excited she could hardly focus on her work. When she looked at the calendar on her desk, the date brought her back to earth, a little calmer, but still happy. It was hump day and the weekend was coming up fast, which meant that she and Ms. Elly would make their weekly visit to the farmers market. Despite all the other memories that Alzheimer's had taken from Ms. Elly, it had not disturbed her memory of the open markets. Before old age had set in Elly and her husband had farmed the land behind their house. Every fall they would take the harvest to the farmers market. Aisha remembered Rodney talking about the trips, with disgust. He hated it. But Aisha was all city-girl and she loved the novelty of it.

Saturday came and just as Aisha thought, Ms. Elly remembered that the girl in the champagne car was coming to take her to the market. The nurse waiting with her had had an ear full of about the market, and was ready to hand over her charge as soon as Aisha walked in. Ms. Elly was cute in her favorite red coat and plaid wool skirt. It remembered Aisha of their time together in years past. It reminded Aisha of their time together in years past.

Delivery

Ms. Shirley Harris was good for showing up at worse times. No matter if she telephoned or suddenly appeared on Aisha's doorstep, it was always a bad time. This Saturday afternoon was no different, except she surprised Aisha by not nagging her about the way she lived. She actually helped with the spring cleaning. Then, to top it off, Ms. Shirley told Aisha that she was coming to Sunday dinner, before they got the got in to a fight. The day left Aisha unnerved. They never got along. They had not been able to share the same space without arguing since Aisha was ten. Something was going to go wrong. An ill wind was headed her way. She could feel it. But she still had things to do.

She was so caught up in the hum of the vacuum that she almost didn't hear the doorbell ring. When she opened the door, she saw a man in a dark suit standing on her front porch.

"Ms. Aisha Harris?"

"Who's asking?"

The man handed her a legal sized envelope. Aisha's toes went cold at the sight of it. She had seen that kind of legal document at a law firm she had once worked for temporarily.

"Ms. Harris, you have been subpoenaed."

It would have been better if the ground had opened and swallowed her whole, instead of having to hear those words. Subpoena equaled every negative thing her mother had ever said to her. The backlash hit her like a wave. She was not the only one who would be affected if she had to go up the river. What about Miss Elly? Who would sit with her on Sunday afternoons and read the paper? Or take her to the farmers market? Who could take in Doris and shell? These thoughts and fears raced through Aisha's mind. It wasn't just a court summons; it was more like a death sentence.

Once the envelope rested in Aisha's hands, the courier walked back to his vehicle, turning a deaf ear to the flow of profanity that spilled from Aisha's mouth. She might look like a lady, but at that moment she sounded like a sailor. She closed the door and pounded into the kitchen, hunting the cabinets for the hidden bottle of *Patron reserve.* Seated at the kitchen table, she went over the events of the last year—the choices she had made, the actions she had taken. It all came to one conclusion; she hadn't done enough. Millie was right. Her friend did not come with benefits. But she hadn't expected any favors, just a good lay. Her first and third shot came and went before she was able to open the envelope. It took two more before she was able to read the document inside. It was worse than she had expected. To be indicted was one thing, but to be called as a witness was another. Ratting out even the lowest cronies was not a good idea. Besides, it was beneath her. They were all hustlers, angling to get ahead, and stay out of each others' way. As she continued to drink, questions arose in her head. How the hell did she get on fedar? And why would she be so damn important? Simple. She knew all those jokers.

She didn't hear Millie drive into the garage. She didn't hear the basement door open or Millie calling out to see if she was home.

"Aisha! Doris! Shell? " Neither dog nor human answered her call. The house was dark and the vacuum cleaning was sitting in the middle of the living room floor.

Millie looked out the patio door. The dogs were locked in their kennel. The Cadillac was parked. Aisha had to be home. Something wasn't right. Millie was about to go searching through the house when she heard a sob from the kitchen. Turning cautiously, Millie spotted Aisha, her head bowed over a shot glass full of Tequila.

Aisha groaned as Millie got her back up into a sitting position. As her eyes adjusted to the light, she almost cried. "Oh, Miss Celie, I's goin' ta jail." Aisha downed the shot then, poured herself another shot.

Millie was stupefied. She knew it had to bad if Aisha was talking like she was in, *The Color Purple*. As Aisha brought the drink to her lips, Millie noticed the letter under her arm. "What is this?" Millie retrieved the document and began to examine it. Aisha poured another shot. It was not as bad as she thought. The word indictment, did not appear anywhere on the page. But to be called to the witness stand was probably just as bad for

Aisha. Millie sat beside Aisha and tried to take the tequila away.

"What I's gon' do?"

"Aisha, listen to me." Millie wasn't sure what to say at first, but then the words started coming out. "You cannot perjure yourself, nor can you talk about what these fools do in their spare time. Remember, you are just a witness, so you only have to attest to what you have seen. Everything else you think you know, or have heard, is hearsay. Testimony like that will just get you and others in trouble."

"Huh?"

"What? Just because I read all day doesn't mean I read junk. Some of my clients are legal eagles. Come on. Get up. Your date with José is over."

"It's *Patron.*"

"Whoever, let's go. I'll bring the children in later."

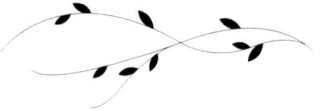

A month later, the court date arrived and Aisha was without her preferred support. Patches was on a tour and Millie was at some conference, leaving only Miss Shirley for her to lean on. As mother and daughter, they had developed a much better relationship in that month, which allowed Aisha to do a lot soul searching and reconciling to prepare for what might happen. Reflecting on the past few days, she could not shake the feeling that she would be getting bad news, no matter what happened on the stand. She had put Shell and Doris in the kennel of the same associate who had found her wonder dog, with instruction if she didn't come back. She had to be ready for anything. Millie was on standby if she was indicted and sentenced after her testimony. Her job would be to keep up the house and carry out Ms. Elly's living will.

The courthouse was a domineering gray building. Aisha prayed for strenght as she proceeded inside. The dark wood of the foyer made her future seem dimmer, and she struggled to find the light at the end of the tunnel. After joining the herd of people being funneled through the security point, she looked around for the bailiff. When she found one, he escorted her into the waiting room until it was her turn to take he stand. Time passed slowly in the little room. She wanted something to drink, but she wasn't allowed outside, and all she had seen on the way in was a fountain in the hall. Sneaking out for a quick sip had crossed her mind a half dozen times before the clock said she had been there ten minutes. But she quieted the urge and sat still in one of the aluminum chairs. The hours crept by before the bailiff returned to take her into the courtroom.

She finally got her sip of water, but it didn't help. The doors opened. Aisha felt as if she were being attacked by the people inside, and the gleam of high-voltage lights on mahogany. She took a step back, but the hand on her shoulder urged her forward. Using the witness stand as a focal, she thought of it as a magnet drawing her in. Sworn in, she took her seat. She surveyed the room before the attorney began. That was enough time to identify half a dozen faces she wished could erase from her memory. It was too late for that. They were all going down. She and Baja made eye contact, and his characteristic golden grin guided her line of sight to a sick-looking inmate being escorted out. The man walking leaving the room was her ex. The joker who started it all, Rodney. Baja mouthed to her, "You're straight," and turned back around to converse with his lawyer. No else seemed to notice this little exchange.

So it was that fool Rodney who had ratted everyone out. Why? Was the pen getting to be too much after eight years? Had the feds offered him a deal? She held on to what to Ms. Shirley and Millie had said: give straight answers, no more, no less. The lawyer began, he asked her to state her full name, and it went downhill from there.

"Do you recognize the defendants, Miss. Harris?"

"Yes."

"Where have you seen them?"

"At parties."

"What kind of parties?"

"A party. A gathering of friends and associates"

"We are all acquainted with the definition. What we want to know is what kind of activities took place at these parties."

Aisha tensed up. "Dancing, card playing, drinking...."

The lawyer cut in. "Were there dog fights, Miss Harris?"

"Yes."

"Were Mr. Bartholomew Jackson, also know as Baja, and his co-defendants promoters of these events?"

"I've known Mr. Jackson to host a variety of private events." She mentally kicked herself for saying too much.

"Private events, you say? Then is it to be our understanding that these parties were by invitation only. You are an accountant and financial advisor. Is that correct? Thus the court can assume you are associated with him on that level, as well? Why else would you be invited to VIP events unless you are providing him with your services?"

"Wait a minute!" She burst out at the same time the defense objected.

The judge struck the gavel and gave the prosecutor a warning before instructing Aisha to answer the first question. She was fuming, but she answered in the must level tone she could achieve.

"Yes I am CPA. No, I don't know what Baj—Mr. Jackson's actual profession is, and I don't know what his books look like. I know some of the co-defendants because we went to high school together. The others lived in the old neighborhood. But I don't hang out with them on a regular basis. The only reason I am acquainted with Mr. Jackson is because of a mutual associate. Does that answer all of your questions Mr. Prosecutor?"

The attorney took his time to respond, picking out another question from his notes. "Would you please tell the court the name of the person that introduced you to Mr. Jackson?"

"Rodney Watson", she replied without hesitation.

"How do you know Mr. Watson, Miss Harris?"

"We were lovers, before his incarceration."

Aisha had no moral qualms about sending Rodney back up. So the Prosecution wanted her to drop a name he would be a first choice every day. He hadn't even bothered to write or call home since. Poor Ms. Elly was all alone.

The lawyer spoke again. "Ah, I see. My sources tell me that you are handling Mrs. Watson's finances. She is currently in a nursing home, correct?"

"Yes. Rolling Green."

"That's an expensive facility. The rent from her property just covers the mortgage. How have you been able to pay for it? Even on your salary, it must be a strain. Perhaps you have a part-time position? Or are you into something more risky"

The defense spoke up. "You're Honor, I object. The witness is not on trial. Miss. Harris is doing a noble thing, taking care of her former lover's ailing mother." The defense was definitely pulling double duty, trying to keep Baja out of jail and keeping the prosecution off Aisha.

The judge agreed and the prosecutor had to back down. Aisha's time on the stand concluded with her being asked to point to anyone in the room she had seen at one of Baja's events. Then she was told she could exit the stand. She was led to another room. A man in a dark suit was waiting for her there.

"Who are you?" she asked.

"I had considered that you wouldn't recognize me."

Ulysses had cut the dreads and goatee and lost the accent.

"Wait a minute," she said. "Shouldn't you be on another assignment by now?"

"Maybe. I just wanted to say that I'm not the one who put you up there. And that that Rodney kid wants talk to you."

The door behind Ulysses opened, and the chained jumpsuit from the courtroom walked in.

Aisha looked Rodney up and down, rolling her eyes.

"Don't be that way Aisha," he said. "I want to thank you for taking care of my mom…."

"Whatever, you snitch. I'm just glad Ms. Elly doesn't remember you."

"That's good. It's better she doesn't have to be sad when I die."

"What bullshit are you talking about? They don't give snitches the chair."

"Naw. It ain't like that. I'm sick. See, I got cancer, and its spreading fast. I don't know how much time I have. I found Jesus. So when they approached me I just told them what I knew. I didn't find out till after the investigation started that you were partying with some of my old friends. Sheltered like you are, you don't know this, but a lot of them are grimy. So please, just be good"

Aisha listened carefully to the words Rodney was choosing. The feds were still listening, and he was trying to protect her. They were all trying to protect her, Patches, Ulysses, Baja, and Rodney. Was she really that much of a troublemaker? Aisha leaned against the wall digesting the situation she was in. It was utter insanity. "I don't mind taking care of Miss Elly," she replied. "She was always sweet to me."

Ulysses coughed to get their attention. "Time to go, Watson. Miss. Harris, I'll be seeing you."

Aisha watched the guards lead Rodney out of the tiny room, unsure whether she felt sad, glad, or angry. Baja had given her a pass, so she there would be no repercussions at home. Rodney was dying and trying to make his peace. Ulysses was making plans to linger in her life. And Patches was probably going to run off with her roommate. Her life had gotten too complicated.

Another bailiff escorted her out of the room and said that she was free to go. Sweeter words had never been spoken.

Fluctuating Movements

There is a good reason they call the weather change of the Pacific Ocean El Niño. It kicks and howls, just like the little boy in seat 9F. However, neither the turbulence in the jet stream nor screaming child inside could disturb the sense of euphoria that enveloped one of the jet's passengers. This elated feeling was a welcomed change after a tension filled week. Millie had been asked, at the last minute to represent the Magazine at a national conference in California. Unfortunately, she been so concerned about the well being of her neighbor that she could hardly focus on the workshops. Thankfully nono of her collegues seemed to notice her lack of interest.

The last day of the conference Millie got a phone call, from Aisha. Aisha let her know that everything had worked out for the better, and that there was no need for her to rush home. Millie shouted hallelujah, the moment she hung up. Which a caused some of the people around her to take extra interest in her. But Millie did not care, she was relieved, and the only thing she wanted right now was a vacation. Standing at the American airline check in desk of LAX, she exchanged her ticket to North Carolina for one to Belize. The name screamed 'vacation, a place to have some me time'.

It started raining the moment she landed. All she could do was laugh, rain was her good omen. An ironic running theme, she had the best experiences when it rained. She enjoyed every minute in Belize, even in the face of a tropical storm. Unlike the other tourists, who had consigned themselves to hotel rooms, Millie found a local watering hole. She spent the entire weekend dancing with the natives.

The night before her excursion ended, the storm moved on. Once the roads and landing strip dried out the jet was able to take off without a hitch into beautiful azure skies. Gazing down at the vanishing land below Millie came to realization, that she should seriously consider a retirement plan to Belize. To live somewhere where the people care and actively protected their eco system; and are genuinely nice, is extremely attractive. But retirement is a long way off and Millie needed to get her head back in work mode. She mediates putting her thoughts in order, waiting for the 'no eletronics' light to off.

When the light does go off she reluctantly pulls a blackberry from her purse. Millie preferred to keep *The Thing,* as she liked to call it, turned off as long as possible. She hadn't looked at it once in three days, there wasn't a need to. She had contacted Robert and the office before she left California. Robert was happy with her report. The office had new reviews and technical advise to mull over, everyone was happy. The screen of her inbox indicated that it was full. No surprise there. She liked the feeling of being inaccessible in a downloadable world.

I have this phone-PC to do my job, and have an overpowered dirt bike to make my life easier, but I don't need them. Besides, people just don't seem to realize how disconnected they are from each with all the techno junk in the way. Texting, e-mail, voice mail, it's all so impersonal. Traffic is the only time most people are forced to be conscious of the people around them. No wonder there are so many road rage incidents. It's the consequences of the world we live in.

Thinking about this reminded her that she still had not thanked Deshawn for convincing her to take a computer class. Otherwise she and *the thing* would not have a working relationship. Opening her inbox, she skimmed over the alerts and reviewed messages until she came across an addressshe had not seen in a while.

> Hey Millie,
>
> Long time, no see. Tanya misses you and wants me to tell you that she is going back to school to become a social worker. Funderburke is giving me a position in the sales and marketing division. He says I'm too people-orientated to be kept in the editing department.
>
> Charlene is beginning to act like a decent human being, thanks

to Tanya. Somehow or another, Tanya located her daughter and has gotten them to reconcile. But the son ... well, let's just say he is hung up on the bull their father fed them.

One more thing, Charlene knows a close friend of your painter and has given out your new address to pass along. You might get another special delivery.

Now for the most important news, you need to come back here the first week in October. My African Queen is going to make an honest man out me, finally.

Call us

Deshawn Clemons

Millie closed the window and steeled heart against the unattainable possibility. The odds were too slim that, Taylar would come back into her life like a welcomed spring breeze. Only for the departure to feel like a gale-force wind, uprooting her stable and suppressed heart. But wasn't that why she had done all of this in the name of the unknown, with the faint hope of seeing that person one more time. Her mission had been to find out if she had grown beyond the scared girl in the painting. She only had two fears left. The first was she had not grown. The second was that Taylar would scuff at all of her efforts. It was too much to think about. She had work to do.

She landed in her new home town without any problems or delays. It seemed odd. The speed at which she had traveled invoked the feeling that fate was rushing her home. Even the cabbie seemed to be flying through the city. Perhaps it was all the good news she had received on the way back, or the end of a wonderful three-day weekend. She had been traveling steadily for over a year, so the magazine would have plenty of material. In between, she had to edit all the incoming articles, so sleep had become a low priority. And church attendance seemed to happen every day but Sunday, though when in doubt, she always had her prayer mat, a gift from Valeria (she was just as unconventional and sweet as Deshawn had described her). This whirlwind life style was tiring at times, but Millie would not trade it.

The cab pulled up to the townhouse, and she rolled her suitcase up the steps, the door opened. Apparently Apparently Millie was not moving fast enough, because Aisha had pulled her into foyer before she could say hello.

"You have a visitor in your room." The way she said it unnerved Millie. She was preparing her mouth to ask who was visiting, but Aisha beat her to it. "That person … is indescribable."

It took every once of will power to keep Millie from running downstairs, but nothing could stop her from becoming watery eyed as she made her way into the basement. The mounting fear that gripped her chest made her stop and breathe. What if whoever was waiting for her was not that person? She would look so foolish. But what if it was that person? What should she say? She kept walking. She took another deep breath.

In a cozy corner constructed out of bookcases and hanging art, Taylar had settled into her favorite chair. Every light seemed to burn ultra-bright, making it easier for Millie to admire the black head bowed over her journal. She stood still, as a statue, watching the scene unfold. Taylar didn't seem to notice her. She should just say 'hello' or 'long time no see'. However, all of those conventional greetings just seemed unbefitting. Without warning Taylar flipped to a dog-eared page and began to read aloud:

> When I look into the mirror I want it to crack. I want it to fall and shatter into a million pieces to pierce my bare feet. When I look into mirror, I see all the horrors in the world. I see what trying to hide from them has made. When I look into the mirror, I feel cold and bitter. I feel as if I should turn my head and pretend it isn't there. When I look into the mirror, I think hardships and simple pleasures make the world worthwhile. I think sometimes it is all too much. When I look into the mirror, I wonder how I fit into

this tangled web of life. How do any of us? When I look in the mirror, I hope that our knowledge and technology don't get the better of us. I hope the world turns out the way that dreamers dream. When I look in the mirror, I wish for things I deem unworthy and impossible. I wish…. I don't know what I wish.

By the time Taylar finished reading the passage, Millie had moved to the ottoman in front of the chair. Setting the book aside, the artist pinned her in place with a warm gaze. "I hope you don't mind," Taylar said. "I didn't realize it was a journal till I was a few pages in."

"It's all right. I only write in it to leave proof of my current existence." She was suddenly twenty-six again and smitten by those chocolate almond eyes.

"I heard you where looking for me," he said. "Since I was passing thru, I thought I'd stop by. Tell me, what made you write such a melancholy prose?"

"I wrote it after I studied the portrait you sent me."

Her response caused Taylar to shift uneasily in the oversized chair. "I barely remember painting it. I found it while I was cleaning out my friend's attic. It took me an entire summer to remember you. I thought you should have it."

Millie waved it off. Someone who didn't know Taylar would have been hurt. "It was months before I opened the package," she said, "and after that, my life seems to have changed. But I don't think I was looking for you. I was looking for myself."

"What did you find?"

"I found that world can be explored by anyone willing to step outside their box. Taylar, what is your favorite color?

"Black. Why?"

"I can spot your work in a dark, crowded novelty shop in Vancouver, but I don't know anything about you."

"Oh. What else do you want to know?"

"Why did you leave the Savannah project?

"You mean the traveling circus? I'm sorry. The revolutionaries were boring. Besides, I found my biological mother, and decided to hop a plane to Nicaragua. And, my friend let me tell you, I understand completely why she dropped me into the hands of the Niancas. I still can't believe they are truly related to me, they're my second cousins, actually. Not that it makes me like them any better."

Millie was mesmerized. Taylar hadn't said anything profound or inspiring, but the air around them had changed. It was alive and tangible. It smelled like amber and sage.

"I don't remember you being so talkative," she finally said.

"And I don't remember you being so open-minded."

"Then I guess we've both changed."

Taylar smiled. "Do you drink coffee? Let me make a pot for you, the Mexican way, or so I'm told. Ground coffee mixed with cinnamon as its percolates. Is your coffee maker in this cabinet?"

Millie nodded and let Taylar search her makeshift kitchenette and make coffee. As the coffee maker on the baker's rack, she asked, "Taylar, why did you paint me?"

The artist did not answer her at first, but filled the pot with water from a 3 gallon container on a baker's rack. Then located cinnamon and coffee (There was cinnamon, thanks to Millie's hobby of making herbal tea). Once the pot began to drip, Taylar returned to the chair. She waited patiently for the contemplative look on her idol's face to vanish.

"Good question," came a quiet voice. "I guess it was because I couldn't get the image out of my head. I saw you before we were introduced. You had just entered the gallery. The seconds between you crossing the threshold and viewing the first piece … the look in your eyes … it—I don't know if anyone else noticed, or that you even knew you could look that way. The look in your eyes, I wanted to know if I had the skill to capture that look."

The coffee was brewed and Millie filled their cups. "Tell me," she said, "how you did it?"

They talked for hours about painting techniques, work projects, people, places, and things. Taylar revealed one layer after another of personal information that Millie drank in happily. This went on long into the night, but when the conversation began to thin, Millie noticed that Taylar was beginning to disconnect. However, she was not ready to let go. A quiet invitation to stay the night was followed by a convenient excuse that it was too late to wake someone else up or travel again swayed her guest. Taylar sat stark still eyeing the duffel near the garage door. "I'll stay if you're okay with sharing."

The night was not supposed to end this way. It was not supposed to end with me lying curled next Millie. I'm not supposed to be dreaming blissfully, holding hands, not wanting to leave. This was not on the program. But some how it's alright to be here with her and feel this connected to someone. Even with Kayla and Ulysses, it wasn't like this. But what does that really mean, connected?

Millie was like twining ivy in Taylar's mind, bringing together abstract thoughts and colors, forming elaborate tapestries that needed to be brought to life. The person, who had been an idle thought, was so inspiring in the flesh. As they slept, their hands had interlocked like two creeper plants tangled in a tropical canopy. Two entities combined, yet independent, growing into and around each other until one snaps to branch off in another direction.

She had asked many questions about Taylar's past, about the comings and goings of people and places. Who was important, and why. But she didn't ask the one question, must people asked or assumed quickly. She just accepted, accepted Taylar, wholly just like Uncle Maurice. He would always give Taylar this kernel of wisdom: It doesn't matter if you wear a dress or suit in this world as long you remember that The Man Upstairs is in charge, and stick to the golden rule. After that everything else is a cake walk.

That was one of the many pearls of wisdom written in Taylar's notebook. A book just like Millie's, proof of Taylar ever changing life. Carefully, quietly Taylar pulled away, to study Millie's journal, again. Her journal was an unpretentious account of a woman exploring herself and the world around her. There was no logical reason to take Millie's journal. Except that, the artist wanted desperately to keep something of the muse near. But taking it would be rude and ripping out a few pages would be worse. Taylar fondled the stems before tucking it into the oversized duffel. The pale light on the patio announced the coming of dawn. It was time go.

Millie knew the moment Taylar pulled away. Watching through half-open eyes, she saw Taylar take her journal. She didn't say anything, until Taylar pulled on a jacket.

"Is it that time already?" she asked from bed, untangling herself from the sheets.

"I didn't mean to wake you, but I have to catch a plane. There is a project I'm working on in New York. When it's done, I'll try to come back here."

Millie felt herself warm as the prospect of another moment like this. But quickly shoved that thought away. Abruptly she crossed the room the stand eye to eye with Taylar.

"Taylar, if you have to go, it's okay. You don't owe me anything, not even an empty promise that you'll come back. The fact that you came means the world to me."

Millie's frankness stunned the artist. Years ago she would have asked for a reliable means of communication. But not now, she did not need to lean on others to experience life. Unable to communicate verbally Taylar embraced her, glad to know another free spirit, and after a long pause said,"I think I love you."

Millie felt juvenile in her mental quest for something to say. Their relationship was real, past and present. She could try to hold on to these fleeting moments or choose to let go. Holding on would smother Taylar, and the artist would rage against her. The right thing to do would be to let go and preserve the memory. "Can I take you to the airport?"

"I would like that."

She drove back to the townhouse with a smile on her face. As she pulled into the garage, she realized that this year had given her some of the most exciting days of her life. She felt free and inspired, just as she had during the mornings she had spent on the roof Deshawn's (and Valeria's) loft. Pulling out her key, she walked into her basement suite and began evaluating the items that she felt defined her life. But nothing stood out. Nothing seemed to embody what was truly important. Her eyes ventured to the portrait that had started her journey, but the emotions it once inspired did so no more. And what did that mean for Millie? Several things, one that she accomplished her goals. Second, it meant that she did not need things to define who she was. Touching the bed and shaking off the euphoria that she had lain there with Taylar, she knew she was complete. She was everything she needed to be, not the naïve, restricted girl in the picture. She and the person she admired most had bonded.

And on top of that she was happy with every aspect of her life.

It was lovely spring day, and she wanted to enjoy every minute of it. First, she had to get some breakfast. Leaping up the stairs, she found Aisha sitting at the breakfast nook.

"You look happy," her landlady said, looking up from a stack of papers. "Is it because you got to see your friend?"

"Yes."

"So is this relationship going to change what's going on with you and my cousin? Patches is all man. Competing with an artistic enigma is not going to go over well."

Millie laughed, but it came out more like a snort. "No, the love I have for Taylar is different. I don't need Taylar here to know that we're connected. My relationship with Patrick is yet to be defined. By the way, how is your *friend?*"

Aisha put down her papers to look Millie in the eye, "To be honest with ya, some things are better let alone. We have no business messing around with each other. But he won't go way and I'm not sure I want him to leave. He saw Taylar yesterday, and from his reaction, I think they know each other. But he won't tell me how."

"And he probably will never tell anyone, about his experience with Taylar. Knowing someone like Taylar can make a person greedy. You don't want to share. All you want to do is be with them, and love them in every possible way. The over load of emotions can be destructive. He probably did something he not to proud of."

Aisha's jaw dropped, "So that wasn't a -"

"SHH!" Millie cut of her landlady quickly. "None of us really knows, and we don't care, Taylar is Taylar."

Aisha dropped the subject. She had only briefly interacted with the artist and found it better to adopt the Taylar fan club sentiment.

"Ok, moving right along, I forgot to tell you, Doris is pregnant. Also, I was kind of hoping you would renew our contract. Not that I need you stay, since I'm going to try living the good life"

"Congratulations on the pregnancy. I hope you find that living on the straight, and narrow can have its benefits."

"But a little risk isn't all that bad, either."

Lightning Source UK Ltd.
Milton Keynes UK
UKOW02f1054261016
286179UK00001B/6/P